Laughing Buddha

a novel by

David G. Lanoue

Laughing Buddha

Red Moon Press
P.O. Box 2461
Winchester VA
22604-1661 USA
redmoon@shentel.net

Cover Painting:
Bertha Lum, *The Homecoming* (1905)
Color Woodcut, 9" x 3.375".
Minneapolis Institute of Arts.
Used with permission.

A Soffietto Edition

for Charles, Randy,
Patrice and Michele . . .
now everyone knows

Laughing Buddha

PART ONE

THE ECLIPSE

IN OLD JAPAN the calendar was timed so that every year on the 15th day of Eighth Month, the harvest moon—that is, the full, radiant moon of the autumn equinox—presided over sacred agricultural rites. On this most auspicious night, farmers set out dumplings, sweet potatoes, and sprays of grasses as offerings to the moon, whom they considered a *kami-sama*, a god. Poets especially loved to come together on this occasion to guzzle sake and scribble in their journals the one-breath poetry of haiku.

All the above I learned in my reading of *Buck-Teeth's Diary*—one of the most famous haiku journals of all time. In that book, Buck-Teeth recounts how he and other literary luminaries gathered one unforgettable night in the mountains of Shinano Province to watch a harvest moon. But soon after moonrise, to everyone's horror, it darkened to total, black eclipse.

Imagine my surprise, then, when just the other night the Channel Six weather guy let slip at the close of an ordinary late September forecast for New Orleans—"muggy and hot"—that a lunar eclipse would happen in twenty four hours, then adding, his eyes strangely intense as if peering at me personally through my twenty-inch screen: "And tomorrow's eclipse will be an exceedingly rare one, it being a harvest moon."

I sat there, stunned.

Before the break to commercial, I had already made up my mind. A shiver of anticipation wriggled up my spine and set my scalp a-tingling. Tomorrow evening, weather permitting, I would drink in with my own two eyes exactly what Buck-Teeth and his cronies had drunk in, so long ago, with theirs! Not only that, but I'd bring along my trusty haiku pad and pen. And then, though we might be separated by a vast gulf of time and space, I could nevertheless be right there, shoulder-to-shoulder with Buck-Teeth and pals, nestled inside the very same experience, scribbling my own one-breath, three-line haiku.

I could hardly wait.

* * *

NEXT NIGHT, I chose as my eclipse-gazing site an outdoor café adjoining the Canal Street ferryboat station. Eager to limber up my poetic muscles, I settled at a river-facing table and flipped open my hip-pocket notepad. I grabbed my roller pen, ready to roll. I ordered a beer, watched, and waited.

A cloud, flickering with lightning, stayed mercifully low and distant. I raised my glass and toasted that cloud, gratefully.

"Kampai!" I gulped. This toast led to others. I toasted the moon, the dark, shimmering river...and one lone tugboat that was pushing a barge upstream toward the Twin Span dotted with lights.

And then, right on time, the moon lost an edge. I raised my pen…

* * *

BACK IN OLD JAPAN, the boys were cranking out haiku, the harvest moon eclipse whipping their creative juices to a froth. Cup-of-Tea, Buck-Teeth's master, bent over his rice-paper diary and drew with wet, dancing squiggles:

world of man!
even the moon
must suffer

Kuro, a somber Poet in Black, wrote an appropriately dark haiku:

the moon and I
sink1ing
to eclipse

Buck-Teeth, meanwhile, struck a brighter chord on the pale page of his destined-to-be-famous diary:

she cools her sunburnt
face...
moon

Also sitting on the poet-clogged verandah was Shiro, all in white. But he only imagined his poem. As always, he tastefully left the paper blank.

* * *

As DID I. Yet, unfortunately, unlike Shiro my blank page was not at all by design. I sat and chewed my pen, waiting for inspiration to strike. It didn't.

But why? For over two years now, ever since I first caught the haiku bug and started writing them day and night, I had done so effortlessly, passionately, filling one hip-pocket notebook after another with off-the-cuff, one-breath, improvisational blurtings. I never had to struggle to make haiku before; they just came to me, flowing off the tip of my pen like blessings from some Buddha from beyond—a mischievous, happy, playful Buddha who loved to surprise me in the unpredictable twist-and-turn of each little poem.

Now, itching to write, my eyes scanned the last, recent entries in my notepad, and I wondered what had gone wrong. Just the other day, strolling through Audubon Park, poems had popped into my brain and onto the page as if writing themselves:

no direction is wrong
arms
of the oak

old stone bridge
whether I cross it
or not

horseshoe tracks
in the mud—
the day's last ant

I sighed, wondering what had happened. Buck-Teeth, Cup-of-Tea, Kuro, Shiro... they were filling the eclipse night air with haiku fast as they could write them or, in Shiro's case, imagine them. But I, though I now saw exactly what they were seeing, had gone completely blank.

Why?

I chugged my beer, slammed a tip on the table, unlocked my bike, hopped on and headed home, disgusted, my mood as dark as the city.

BUCK-TEETH'S SILENCE

FROM THE MORNING he became Cup-of-Tea's haiku apprentice in misty Kashiwabara village, until the night six decades later when the Buddha stopped dreaming him, Buck-Teeth recorded his poetry and life in a fat, rice-paper diary. However, a conspicuous gap exists in this almost lifelong chronicle. For four and a half months, he wrote absolutely nothing in his wonderful book. After his haiku on the night of the eclipse—the one about the moon cooling her sunburnt face—a blank page follows. And then, on the next page, in an entry dated exactly 130 days later, he resumes:

New Year's Day. Fujikawa. Clear and cold.

> A perfect morning for haiku—alive again! Kuro, Shiro and Kojiki left this morning, heading back to Edo. But I've decided to linger a while on this icy toe of the sacred mountain.

Village children, running and laughing, even now fly their New Year's kites.

living dangerously
the kite skims
the river

...and from that point on, for the rest of his life, Buck-Teeth faithfully added to the diary, every day—a fact that makes the 130 day gap in it all the more glaring. Why did he quit haiku for such a long spell? Was he suffering from writer's block, perhaps? Or had he decided to emulate, for a season, the silent poetry of the ever-silent Shiro? And when he finally got back down to the business of haiku that New Year's morning, whatever did he mean by the cryptic exclamation, "Alive again!"?

When I first read *Buck-Teeth's Diary*, I was mystified by its four-and-a-half month gap. The fact that it began the day after the harvest moon eclipse struck me as particularly odd. How could he fail to be inspired, waking up that next morning in the august company of Shiro, Kuro, and Cup-of-Tea?

Just as strangely, after 130 days of hiatus he picked up his bamboo brush and let loose a poetic avalanche that roared on unabated, day by day and page after page, until his death forty years later. I wondered: What had inspired him to re-launch his haiku career with such exuberant and unstoppable momentum? In light of my own recent failure to produce a single haiku on eclipse night, this question had special, personal import.

Yearning for an answer, I decided to pay a visit to a local expert on the subject: Professor Nakamura, the distinguished chair of Uptown University's Asian Languages and Literatures Department. His book of haiku criticism—700 pages of small, academic print—convinced me: if anyone knew the why and wherefore of Buck-Teeth's poetic silence, it would be Nakamura.

"Professor," I said after I entered his office, bowing the way I had learned to do during my summer in Japan, "It's so nice of you to see me."

He didn't bow but instead shook my hand Western-style. He looked younger than I had expected. Sprinkles of gray lightened his black, short-cropped hair, but his face, especially his eyes, brimmed with fierce energy.

"Please, be seated," he said.

I sat. The professor, with lithe steps, circled his desk and slid into a large black leather power chair. A sleek, jet-black computer gleamed on the desk between us, next to a single cut lily in a clear glass vase. A giant wall map of the Japanese islands—lime green with thousands of tiny, handwritten scribbles in red—loomed behind the world-famous scholar.

After some small talk about the financial crisis in Asia, we got down to business.

"I'm interested in the poet Buck-Teeth, professor. You've written a lot about him," I said.

"Ah, yes, Buck-Teeth."

"He's one of my favorites, too. I think he's great."

"The *early* Buck-Teeth, perhaps."

I shrugged. I was aware of the professor's theory that haiku as a literary form had hit its peak in Buck-Teeth's youth and ever since had been in decline. But I wasn't there for a debate, so I let his comment slide. I continued. "I'm curious about a certain puzzle in *Buck-Teeth's Diary*."

He frowned, said nothing.

I cleared my throat. "You see, I'm writing a book—"

"So that's your game, is it?" he snapped. "You have a lot of nerve, coming here!"

I was baffled by this outburst and by the sudden bright flush in the professor's cheeks. I stammered, "If you could just, uh, enlighten me about—"

He raised an index finger to his lips. "I think you should leave."

"But—"

"Now!" he hissed. "Good day!"

I stood to go. Professor Nakamura remained

seated. No handshake now. His eyes held me in a cold, angry glare.

"Good day," I mumbled and left, wondering what the hell had just happened.

* * *

After that weirdness in Professor Nakamura's office, I didn't know what to do. Without expert help, how was I ever going to solve the riddle of Buck-Teeth's poetic silence?

I pondered this dilemma all the next afternoon as I sat in my neighborhood pub, sipping big frosted goblets of Happy Hour beer. Why had Buck-Teeth quit writing for so long? This was way out of character for the village poet, Cup-of-Tea's most brilliant student, who went on to gain fame, if not fortune, in the haiku world. I wondered: Who on earth knew the answer to this burning question—among the living, that is? After all, I couldn't exactly ask Buck-Teeth.

Ask Buck-Teeth?

I chuckled. It was a drunken thought, which, like most such thoughts, made perfect sense at the time. Sure...why not? To find out what became of young Buck-Teeth after the eclipse—why he quit haiku and, even more importantly to me, what motivated him four and a half months later to take it up again—I'd go straight to the source. I didn't own a time machine, at least not of the H. G. Wells variety, but I did have in my possession something just as good for the purpose: my blue Bic roller pen. Through the ineffable power of this sacred object I could easily, instantly, travel to Buck-Teeth's world, to Old Japan, traversing time and space, writing myself, body and mind, into this very book! And then, in a matter of mere pages, I could be standing toe-to-toe with Buck-Teeth, asking questions to my heart's content, recording his answers verbatim.

It was a plan.

But before I could put it into action, I needed a disguise that would allow me to hobnob with folks of that long-ago era without raising their eyebrows. I pondered and drank.

A beer and a half later, I had it, the perfect solution: I'd pose as a wandering Buddhist priest, a rootless holy man. I'd have to shave myself bald—not much effort, there—and swaddle myself in a baggy saffron robe. Excellent! But there was a catch: I didn't relish the thought of traipsing about Old Japan in the stiff straw clogs of the period. So, for comfort's sake, I decided to keep my well-worn, blue-and-white Reeboks. My priestly robe would just have to dangle low enough to the ground to hide my anachronistic sneakers.

My identity and costume established, I was all set. My heart beat faster. I was about to meet, in person, the giants of one-breath verse: Cup-of-Tea, Kuro, Shiro, Buck-Teeth! I felt like a secret agent setting off on a mission under deep cover, on my way to an exotic land filled with sex and violence and haiku: the Old Japan of geisha, samurai, and mad, moonstruck poets.

JAPAN

I MATERIALIZED in rushes behind the house of Inacho, the sake brewer, where, according to *Buck-Teeth's Diary*, the harvest moon eclipse-viewing party had taken place just the night before. My Reeboks sank into soft, swampy muck. It was dawn in Old Japan, cool and misty. In the haze a flock of wild geese, startled by my appearance, took off, honking and flapping.

"Saraba, saraba!" I bid the geese farewell, reveling in my sudden knowledge and flawless pronunciation of the old dialect.

And then, inspired, I babbled into the mist my very first Japanese haiku:

aki kaze ya
ukiyo no kari wa
ukare keri

. . . which, in English, roughly translates to:

autumn wind—
the floating world's geese
afloat

My newfound fluency in Japanese was intoxicating, but I felt even more elated at how effortlessly the haiku had flowed from mind to mouth to misty morning air. The mental block that had prevented my composing a single eclipse poem the other night seemed to have completely melted away. My trip to Old Japan was starting off splendidly!

Slogging through squishy mud, I reached Inacho's house, rimmed by a wide, covered verandah. Stepping onto that verandah, I spotted abundant remnants of last night's moon party: tatami mats, tobacco trays, and sake cups, most of the latter empty but a few containing vestiges of a clear liquid. I lifted one and sniffed. It smelled like a mixture of vodka and gasoline.

I set the cup down, carefully, on the dew-slicked verandah.

"Good morning!" A gruff voice startled me. I whirled about-face to find a short, stocky man standing there, his bright red *yukata* robe open at the chest.

"Good morning to you," I said, bowing.

The stocky man bowed, too, flashing a bald spot.

"I'm sorry to intrude so early in the day," I said.

"But I seek an old friend, a poet who goes by the name of Buck-Teeth."

"Ah, but you're too late, priest. By the way, I'm Inacho. And you would be...?"

I didn't know what to answer. In my haste to get to Old Japan, I had neglected to prepare a name for my priestly self.

"Me? I, uh, I'm called..." My eyes scoured the scene, desperate for inspiration, but all I saw were the rushes, the mist, and, looking down...

Mud. *Doro* in Japanese.

"Doro-bô?" I muttered.

"Priest Mud?" He frowned. I had picked an odd one, but there was no fixing it now.

"Yes. That's it. That's my name. But back to Buck-Teeth. Surely he hasn't left already?"

Inacho shrugged his broad shoulders. "Ah, but sadly, he has. He and his master, Cup-of-Tea, departed early—on their way to Jokyô Temple, they said. You know the place?"

"Uh, I'm not familiar with the *local* temples."

"No matter. I have guests going there later today. Perhaps you could accompany them. It isn't far."

"Thank you for your kindness!" I bowed. He bowed. I bowed again. He bowed again. Unsure of the protocol of the period, I bowed a third time, but Inacho matched me. Who was supposed to have the last bow? There was so much about Old Japan that I simply didn't know!

Before I could drop my head for number four, a dark figure strode out of the house. He was tall and gaunt with a stark, angular face; a large, square forehead; a high top-knot of salt-and-peppered hair. A midnight black *yukata* hung on his bony frame.

It was Kuro in the flesh!

"Kuro," I gushed, bowing, "What an honor it is to meet you!"

"You know me, priest?" The Poet in Black sounded suspicious.

"I, uh, yes, well...I've heard of you. I mean, who hasn't heard of Cup-of-Tea's haiku students, each of you wearing his color, and each a master in his own right?"

The flattery worked. Kuro—ever so slightly—grinned.

Just then Shiro stepped out of the house, his mouth falling open with surprise at Kuro's rare smile. I was surprised, too, but for a different reason. Shiro's robe was not nearly as pristinely white as I had imagined it would be. In fact, it was drab off-white at best, with muddy streaks and splotches around the legs. Clearly, Old Japan could have used our modern laundry detergents with their whiteners, brighteners, and stain-attacking enzymes.

Inacho spoke. "Priest Mud here is a friend of Buck-Teeth's but doesn't know the way to Jokyô-ji. I thought that, perhaps—"

"Of course," Kuro interrupted, then addressed me. "You may come with us, if you like."

"That's so kind of you!"

"Think nothing of it," Kuro said. Shiro nodded, grinning hugely.

Inacho invited us to join him for breakfast. The Poet in Black and the Poet in White [that is, Off-White] reentered the house. I started to follow but at the threshold remembered that decorum required me to remove my footwear. I froze.

"Please," Inacho gestured to the open door.

I sighed. Why hadn't I anticipated this situation when I opted to wear the Reeboks? *That's what I get for planning this thing drunk*, I chided myself.

Inacho waited.

Seeing no way around it, I sighed again, then kicked off my big, muddy sneakers, setting them alongside Shiro's and Kuro's straw clogs. Compared to the petite sandals of Old Japan, my size elevens looked gargantuan.

"Unusual shoes," the sake brewer commented.

"I know," I mumbled. "They're from China."

* * *

After a hearty breakfast of thick buckwheat noodles with raw quail eggs swimming in a savory broth, we settled onto straw mats in Inacho's front room, for tea. I was eager to hit the road and catch up with Buck-Teeth, but whenever Kuro's or Shiro's cup emptied, our solicitous host asked, "Won't you have some more?" And, to my dismay, every time, Kuro said, "Yes," and Shiro nodded.

Hours passed.

For the most part I said little, playing my role of otherworldly priest immersed in deep meditations. But then the conversation suddenly steered my way.

"So, have you known our friend Buck-Teeth long?" Inacho inquired.

"Uh, yes. Going on, I'd say, two years."

"Really?" Kuro arched his black eyebrows. "Are you a poet then?"

"I write, a little," I muttered.

Shiro stared at me intently, smiling. He wanted something, but what? Then I understood.

"Oh. You'd like me to recite a haiku of mine?" I asked.

He nodded excitedly.

"OK then. Well, here goes." I thought for a moment and then instantly translated from modern English to Old Japanese a haiku that I had composed just a month earlier on Bourbon Street, after a cloudburst:

shined by the storm
the clip-clopping
mule

Kuro slurped his tea. "Ah, yes. For a fleeting moment the common beast gleams like precious jade."

"That's lovely!" I said, liking Kuro's explication even better than my poem that had inspired it. But Kuro wasn't finished.

"And then, inevitably, the patina of glory fades, and the creature continues its toilsome life only to be rewarded, all too soon, with the utter, empty nothingness of death."

We sat quietly for a long while, staring down at the green tea leaves in the bottoms of our cups. Kuro's bitter philosophizing could really dampen a mood.

Eventually, Shiro cleared his throat; Kuro nodded. They set down their cups.

"Leaving so soon?" Inacho asked.

"Yes, we must be going," Kuro said. "Thank you, my friend, for your hospitality. Last night was quite an affair."

I clicked my own cup onto the lacquered tray. "I thank you, too, Inacho, for a great breakfast...and the tea."

We all stood. After a mad flurry of bows, we exited, single file, to the verandah. Kuro and Shiro stepped into their clogs, swung their weather-beaten satchels over their shoulders, grabbed their bamboo walking sticks. I worked my own feet into my mud-caked Reeboks. More bowing transpired with gusto, everyone spouting, "Farewell! Farewell!"—*saraba, saraba, saraba* over and over—until the Poet in Black, the Poet in White, and I, a saffron-robed priest named Mud, started up the narrow road into steep, misty mountains...on our way at last.

COMPLICATIONS

JOKYÔ TEMPLE wasn't far from Inacho's house, but we didn't arrive there quickly. Quite often along the way, Kuro or Shiro—or both—felt the urge to stop and compose haiku. When Kuro did so, this was especially time-consuming, since he had to wet and grind his ink. And though Shiro's poetry required no ink, brush, or paper, each time he raised his hand to indicate he was imagining one of his nonverbal "dibbits," as Kuro called them, we had to wait a good ten minutes at least. Eventually, though, the gentle hand would fall and a Mona Lisa smile would curve on Shiro's lips, signaling that his silent haiku was done...and we continued our trek.

A breezy day in the autumn mountains, there was plenty to write about—or, for Shiro, not to write about: falling leaves, buzzing dragonflies, the happy clomp-clomping of six human feet. At one point, when the others weren't looking, I scribbled my own impromptu verse on a little pad that I had hidden in the inner folds of my priestly robe:

dragonfly's warm-up stretch
tail up
tail down

I smiled, pleased by my rediscovered poetic fluency—even in English! *Must be the air of this Old Japan*, I mused, breathing it in deeply.

When the shadows of the cedars stretched thick and black across the road, Kuro announced, "We're almost there."

I was thrilled, eager to interrogate Buck-Teeth and solve the mystery that had brought me to his era. My stomach was eager too, growling.

"Will we dine at the temple, then?" I asked in a hopeful tone.

"If we're invited," Kuro said flatly.

And then, suddenly, something felt...not right. Shiro, who had been walking in the lead, froze.

"What is it?" I asked.

We all three stood still in the lengthening shadows, listening to an eerie silence.

"Do you hear that?" Kuro whispered.

"I hear nothing," I said.

"That's just it! No birds. No insects. This is bad."

Shiro, who normally loved peace and quiet, nodded, his eyes wide with concern.

"*Very* bad," Kuro emphasized.

"What is it?" I asked in a low voice.

"I don't know." Kuro looked left, looked right...then looked left again. "I fear...we're being watched."

Being watched? I pondered this for a moment. As characters inside my book, we were of course, all of us, being watched by you, the reader. Yet this fact didn't quite explain the cold, malevolent *presence* that each of us plainly sensed in the quiet autumn dusk.

A twig snapped. Our heads swerved in unison to track the sound. In steep woods forty feet away, something large, inky black, melted into the tree trunk shadows.

"A ninja," Kuro whispered. "I suggest we hurry to the temple!"

Shiro and I agreed. The last half-mile, we jogged.

* * *

"Buck-Teeth and Cup-of-Tea left at noon," the head monk informed us.

I winced. My mission to Old Japan wasn't turning out as smoothly as I had anticipated. Complications were setting in, not the least of which being the fact that a watcher—a dark, gliding ninja—was stalking us. But why? What did a ninja have to do with poets of haiku such as Kuro and Shiro, and a "priest" such as myself?

Kuro shared my puzzlement. He asked the head monk—a small, agreeable fellow—"Are military maneuvers occurring in the district? Earlier, we spotted a ninja."

"None that I know of," the monk replied placidly, then swung his gaze to me. "Greetings, brother. Would you be a follower of Rinzai, Nichiren, Shinran...?"

"Shinran," I said quickly, repeating the only name on the list that I recognized from my reading.

"Shinran? Very good. And your temple?"

"My temple? Uh, it's... far away. You see, I'm a wandering priest."

"Oh?"

"My name is Mud," I added sheepishly.

But the head monk seemed unperturbed by my odd moniker. "Welcome, Priest Mud," he said, bowing deeply. "As a fellow seeker of enlightenment, won't you join us in our unworthy repast? And your companions, too?"

My mouth already watering, I bowed just as deeply and smiled at the ground, glad for my priestly identity. Membership had its privileges.

"If it's not too much trouble," I said.

* * *

THE ANCIENT SPIES of Japan were aptly named. Ninja, literally, means "hider." The ninja's entire profession was hiding: blending in seamlessly with his surroundings to wait and to watch. Often, the goal was strictly reconnaissance. At other times, though, ninja were employed as assassins: artists of knife, noose, and poison.

The particular ninja who tracked us to Jokyô Temple, by ninja standards, was a bungler. A true master of sneaking never would have allowed himself to be seen the way that he had, not even for a second.

Haiku poets can learn much from the ninja. They, too, must glide into scenes with eyes and ears and all senses keenly alert. And then, once in place, the poet, ninja-like, cultivates stillness. Just as Cup-of-Tea taught Buck-Teeth in his earliest lessons, the haikuist must stop, look, and listen before daring to write. Like the ninja, he or she settles into the picture and becomes part of it, ensconced inside it: a spy spying on his/her surroundings and on his/her own self within such surroundings.

In my pre-eclipse days, one-breath poems used to pop into consciousness at any time, in any place. Like the black-garbed hiders of Old Japan, I infiltrated scenes with senses wide open to whatever was... and "whatever was" invariably became haiku. I spied at my job:

foggy campus
the student I failed
walks away

I spied at the art museum:

sculpture garden
Hercules' penis
wins

I spied at the Audubon Zoo:

milkweed fluff in the air
the sleepy
lions

And, of course, I even spied on myself:

mirrors, mirrors
drinking
with my bald spot

Just as the ninja absorbs myriad details to make an accurate report to his samurai commander, the haiku poet, too, must remain ever-vigilant, prepared to reach for pen and paper at a moment's notice, even when awakened in the dead of night:

biting my hand
at two a.m.
ant

* * *

WE STAYED at Jokyô Temple for two whole days. Cold, slashing rain fell all the first day, trapping us inside the dim but cozy main hall. On the second morning, storm clouds again darkened the sky.

"We'd best not risk it," Kuro advised. And the Poet in Black was right; it poured.

I longed to get going and catch up with Buck-Teeth and Cup-of-Tea. But I consoled myself with the thought that they, too, must be holed up in some temple or inn, waiting out the bad weather in the mountains—or so I hoped.

The morning of the third day the sun blazed in clear, azure heavens—praise Buddha! Kuro, Shiro and I bade farewell to the kind monks. We hadn't proceeded far on the mud-slicked road when I asked my monochrome companions, "So, where are you headed?"

"To Edo," Kuro replied. "It's back home for me."

Shiro's nod indicated that he had made the same decision.

This was bad news. According to the monks, Buck-Teeth and Cup-of-Tea were en route to their native village of Kashiwabara. For me to catch up with them, I would need to get to Kashiwabara post-haste. But alone and without a guide, it would be awfully easy to get lost in these mountains.

"Hey, why don't we drop in on dear old Cup-of-Tea?" I suggested.

"But Shiro and I just saw the master," Kuro said.

"Yes, but that's my point! We could all show up on his doorstep and surprise him. He won't be expecting that."

The Poet in Black briefly considered my proposal, then shook his head, *no*. But the Poet in White, smiling broadly, shook his, *yes*.

"No," Kuro said firmly, out loud.

Shiro nodded *yes*, just as firmly.

I broke the stalemate: "I vote we go see Cup-of-Tea."

Shiro smiled. Kuro frowned. But majority ruled. The three of us set off for Kashiwabara. And we made good progress, stopping only once for haiku writing or, in Shiro's case, haiku imagining.

When the sun had ducked behind snow-capped mountains, we crossed a wide, rushing river on a creaking footbridge. On the other side, around a bend, we found a tiny village.

Kuro rapped his stick on the stone-and-dirt main street. "The Shogun's highway," he announced.

"Then is it far to Kashiwabara?" I asked.

"About five *ri*."

I calculated. Five *ri* in the Old Japanese system

equaled twelve miles, give or take. Through steep mountains and in darkness, such a distance would be hard to cover.

Kuro arrived at the same conclusion: "We'll stop here," he said. "There's an inn."

HASUKO

The tea-girl was called Hasuko.

"That's a pretty name," I said. In English, it means, "Lotus Child."

Her burnt orange kimono bore a design of tall, white-petaled blossoms that resembled the sunflowers of my native Midwest. She served us dinner, kneeling close to our table, fawning over me.

"Would you like some more eel, priest?"

"Let me get that for you, priest."

"Such strong hands you have, priest."

After dinner, she left to fetch the sake. I confided to my companions, "She's flirting with me, that girl."

"It's about time you noticed," Kuro remarked.

"But I'm a priest!"

Shiro snickered.

Kuro shook his head with disdain. "Are you not a priest of Shinran's sect?"

"Yes, but—"

"Then what's the problem? Don't you True Teaching Pure Land priests scoff at the idea of sin?"

Kuro was right. In my study of Old Japan, I had stumbled upon the works of Shinran, the Buddhist patriarch who argued that one cannot earn one's salvation. Obeying Buddhist precepts or chanting this or that prayer will only damn a person, in the next life, to the stew-pots of King Emma's hell, Shinran preached. All desire, even the desire to avoid sin in this craven "world of man," is destructive. The only way to enlightenment, to rebirth in the Pure Land in this fallen age, Shinran taught, is to trust utterly in Amida Buddha's saving power.

Before tonight, this teaching had been merely an intellectual curiosity, a vague abstraction. But now that I was physically present in Old Japan, bald and swaddled in priestly garb, the liberating philosophy of Shinran had definite, personal significance.

"You mean, I can sleep with her?" I whispered.

"When she returns," Kuro said in a low voice, "ask if she plays the koto."

Hasuko shuffled back into the room with a tray upon which sat a porcelain pitcher of sake and three small cups. Again, she knelt close to me. The orange silk sleeve of her kimono brushed my arm, raising the hairs with a jolt of erotic electricity. She set down the tray and began pouring.

"None for me, thanks," I said, recalling how deathly potent the leftover rice wine had smelled the other morning on Inacho's verandah. "However," I added, "I was wondering. I mean, I'm curious... Do you happen to play the koto?"

Shiro giggled. Kuro shot him a stern look.

Hasuko, without missing a beat, answered, "My koto is upstairs. If you would do me the honor... "

She handed Shiro and Kuro their drinks and then stood, motioning for me to follow. I did so. We walked around a folding screen that showed a golden autumn landscape, through a narrow doorway, and up a flight of rickety wood steps. When we reached the top, I heard, down below, Shiro's muffled laughter.

She guided me into a little room where a thin futon lay spread over several finely woven straw mats. An anvil-shaped pillow jutted up at one end of the futon. A translucent globe lantern, hanging in the open window, tinted the walls, the bedding, and Hasuko's face green. She slid the door shut behind us.

I smiled, remembering how loudly Chaz of my writing group had complained about the sex scene in my previous book, calling it "sketchy." But this was about to change, I hoped...for his sake and mine.

Hasuko knelt on the quilt. No koto, no Japanese zither, in sight. If there was going to be music in that green-lit room, our bodies would have to make it.

We stripped.

* * *

"May I touch?" she asked politely.

"Yes, touch me," I breathed, kneeling across from her on the quilt, my "jade peak" rising, as they say in Old Japanese pillow books. "Touch me anywhere."

But to my surprise, she ignored the jade peak and instead reached up to my face. Her fingers caressed my cheeks and chin ever-so softly. "Fuzzy!" She laughed like a delighted child.

After several days in Old Japan without razor or shaving cream, my face had indeed grown fuzzy. Whether it was the beard itself or its blondness, Hasuko seemed sexually interested in it. She rubbed her cheeks against it, and then her neck, and then her pretty, pink nipples. The stubble must have tickled; she laughed, brushing various body parts against it.

By now jade peak was urgently ready for misty valley, if you catch my drift. But peak and valley would not meet. A crash and clatter downstairs made Hasuko, green in the lamplight, gasp.

And then another sound: heavy feet stomping, someone bounding up the stairs.

The paper door lurched open. The innkeeper, eyes bulging, thrust his head into the room.

"Your friends," he said, breathlessly, "the fellows in white and black. They're dead!"

* * *

"That can't be!" I dropped my pen. Kuro and Shiro dead?

I jumped up from my writing table, knocking over the chair I had been sitting on. The kitchen floor was cluttered with papers, books, laundry, and maps of Old Japan. I leaped over the mess to the dusty bookshelf in the hall.

Where is it? Where is it? Frantically scanning titles on spines of books, I finally spotted it: a fat paperback with blood-red lettering: Nakamura's *From Basho to Buck-Teeth: Haiku's Rise and Decline*. I knew from my earlier reading of the text that Shiro was not mentioned, an oversight explainable by the fact that Shiro never committed his poetry to paper and so gave critics nothing to critique. Kuro, though, had an entire chapter devoted to him somewhere near the end. Holding my breath, I flipped pages till I found it. My eyes fell on the year of the eclipse. I started reading:

> *The Poet in Black was not immune to the decline of haiku as a form. In fact, one can apply the eclipse of the harvest moon of that autumn metaphorically. In the two unremarkable decades that followed it, Kuro's haiku production dwindled in both quantity and quality, and need not concern us here. The eclipse, indeed, was total.*

I closed the book. I had almost forgotten how cold and prissy Nakamura's tone was, yet, nevertheless, his survey of the haiku masters was painstakingly accurate in its biographical details. In the present case, it was reassuring: Kuro couldn't possibly have died in that inn just now. According to history, he had at least twenty more years to "dwindle"!

I rushed back to the table, righted the toppled chair, and sat. My Bic lay where I had dropped it, midway between coffee mug and a mound of pages covered with blue chicken scratches, this morning's chapter interruptus.

I grabbed my roller pen and started rolling, determined to save my friends.

* * *

THEY LAY with their eyes closed, flat on their backs amid the debris of a shattered sake pitcher. The Poet in Black and Poet in White side by side, motionless.

"Impossible," I muttered as I knelt over them. Their faces were dark purple, the color of rotten plums; their arms and hands ghastly pale. "They can't be—"

"Oh they're dead all right," the innkeeper assured me. "Their necks..."

I bent in closer. Their Adam's apples, flattened, bore hideous bruises, purple as their faces.

"He smashed their windpipes, the shadow warrior did," a large stranger, dressed in the rags of a beggar, reported.

The innkeeper shouted, "I told you to stay out of here!"

"Just trying to help," the beggar whined. "I saw the ninja. I'm a witness. And I'll describe him...for food."

"Out!" The innkeeper pointed to the door, through which the beggar reluctantly skulked.

I stared at the Poets in White and Black, baffled. Shiro, I wasn't sure of, but Kuro was supposed to have twenty more years of life ahead of him, precious years for haiku writing and grumbling about how meaningless everything is.

"He isn't dead," I whispered, stroking his big

square forehead with its deep, philosophical creases. It felt cold...leathery.

And then...

A strange gurgle emanated from deep in Kuro's chest, and air, stinking of stale sake, exploded out his blue lips. Shiro exhaled a second later, coughing loudly. Then the eyes of both "dead" poets popped open wide.

"A miracle!" the innkeeper shouted. He fell to his knees and began chanting, loudly, *"Namu Amida Butsu,"* over and over. I stood and grinned, basking in the power of the pen.

Their complexions improved quickly from purple to pink. They sat up.

"What happened?" Kuro asked, rubbing his throat.

"Are you all right?" I asked.

"Feels like I swallowed glass."

"It was a ninja," I said. "He struck you, both of you."

Shiro massaged his throat too, his usual expression of bemused tranquility replaced by one of eye-bulging terror.

"But why would a ninja attack *us*?" Kuro scrambled to his feet, then helped up his comrade. "Are you certain?"

"That's what the beggar said."

The innkeeper's praising of the Buddha continued unabated. Hasuko, who had taken longer than I to dress, now rushed into the room. Seeing the Black and White Poets upright and alive, she let out a squeal of amazement.

"I'd like to talk to that beggar," Kuro said. "But first, miss..." he addressed Hasuko, "we could use some tea."

KOJIKI

NEXT MORNING, we found the beggar. He wasn't hard to spot: a heap of grungy rags in the alley behind the inn, snoring.

"That's him," I whispered.

Kuro approached and prodded the rag heap with his walking stick, and it galvanized into motion, becoming a gray, rolling blur out of which a bare foot shot in the air, knocking the cane out of Kuro's grasp. It clattered to the ground thirty feet away.

Crouched in a martial arts stance, the beggar gasped, "The dead men!"

"Not dead, my friend," Kuro assured him.

"But I saw you! I saw what he did!"

"That's what we'd like to talk to you about," I said. "Last night you claimed you could describe the person who attacked my friends. He was a ninja, you said?"

The beggar grinned, revealing a missing tooth, a front upper. "For a meal, I'll tell all."

He never mentioned his name, so we called him from that point on, Kojiki, which denotes in Japanese exactly what he was: a "beggar." Over a fine breakfast of rice, miso soup, and cold fish at the inn; Kojiki told his tale, his voice a gruff, vibrant baritone, the esses whistling through the hole where his tooth had been.

* * *

I WASN'T ALWAYS as you s-s-see me now. I was well off once, a samurai in my youth. But I quit the Shogun's honor guard to pursue my dream. I became an actor, and was quite good, I tell you. Ask anyone who knows anything about kabuki!

Before long I was the talk of Edo, a rising star of the stage. There, I put my samurai skills to good use, played the hero in a thousand dramas. Oh how I strutted and swaggered with my sword and fan! I was never happier than in those days.

But the act grew old. No, "stale" is the word. I was fabulously popular but going through the same tired motions. A sword thrust this way. A foot stomp that way. Eyebrow up, eyebrow down. Stale! So I added new little touches here and there, changing this, tweaking that. I was an artist, after all, and art must grow or it dies, am I right?

The audience...they hated it. Hissed at my every new move, demanded to see what they'd come for, what they expected to see. Theater wasn't art for them, just comfortable, familiar spectacle.

The kabuki master warned me to resume my old ways, or else. Of course, I refused.

After that, my roles grew smaller and smaller. No longer the hero, I now played the hungry ghost, the loyal attendant...the old buffoon.

Finally, I quit. And ever since that day I've lived on the open road, wandering this Japan from Kyushu to Hokkaido. But my eyes stay always open; you can be sure of that!

I'm telling you all this so you'll believe me when I say what I saw. I'm a reliable witness. Thanks to my military training, I know all the ways to kill—and how to hide, how to observe the enemy unseen. That ninja was crafty but quite the amateur.

I spotted him right away, creeping in the shadows, peeping through the window while you ate. I had just been escorted out of this fine establishment and was reclining in the street across the way, wondering what I might do to soothe the growling demons in my belly. That's when I saw him.

What did he look like? Well, he looked...like a ninja.

May I have more rice? And how about a cup of sake to wash it down?

* * *

KOJIKI'S VAGUE TESTIMONY was a disappointment, but Shiro paid for the extra rice and sake. I even dared to partake of the latter with small, careful sips. The innkeeper served us, frowning at the beggar. Hasuko was nowhere in sight.

"I still don't understand," Kuro said, "why a ninja would attack poets."

"So you're poets, are you?" Kojiki downed his drink. "That ninja's a bad man, killing poets!"

"We weren't killed," Kuro reminded him.

"Perhaps," Kojiki said.

After just a few sips, the sake was already warming my belly and dizzying my head. The stuff wasn't half bad, after all. I chugged the rest.

"Yee-haw!" I yelped.

Shiro and Kuro shot me the same odd look. I couldn't read their emotion. Was it shock? Sadness?

"What's wrong?" I asked.

"Nothing," Kuro said softly. "It's just...an old friend of ours used to crow when *he* drank."

Shiro nodded, and then I remembered my history: the Poet in Green, Mido—their comrade and fellow disciple of Cup-of-Tea—several years ago drank himself to death or, to state the case more poetically, faded forever from Buddha's dream.

His last dollop of rice gobbled, Kojiki threw down his chopsticks. "You poets, and you, too, priest, you need protection. Persistence is the ninja's code. He'll be back. He'll try again."

Shiro, visibly shaken by the beggar's prediction, finished his sake in a gulp.

"I can protect you," Kojiki said. "Remember, I was a samurai once, and a good one. I know all the deadly arts. I'll see him coming. I'll keep the three of you alive...for food."

Kuro rubbed his chin, considering the offer.

"And a bit of sake, now and then," Kojiki added.

Shiro looked at Kuro pleadingly.

"I don't know..." Kuro said, but Shiro's eyes were unrelenting.

"Well...all right," the Poet in Black sighed.

Later that morning, Shiro, Kuro and I started off for Cup-of-Tea's village in the mountains, accompanied by the ragged, former samurai, former actor, former beggar, present bodyguard, Kojiki. Glancing back over a shoulder, I caught sight of Hasuko in an upstairs window of the inn, staring.

I waved, but she didn't wave back.

MEETING THE MASTER

CUP-OF-TEA'S WIFE, Kiku, opened the soot-blackened door.

Kuro spoke to her, offering greetings and inquiring after the health of her and her husband. My heart hammered wildly. I was about to meet one of the world's greatest poets! Though I had come to Old Japan expressly to see Buck-Teeth, I had as many questions for his master. Interviewing Cup-of-Tea would be, as we say back in New Orleans, wonderful lagniappe.

Kuro introduced me to Kiku: "Chrysanthemum" in Japanese. She looked to be thirty-something, short and stocky with bright eyes under heavy lids, her cheeks full and flushed. Her body animated her plain peach-colored kimono with the robust energy of a peasant daughter of peasants who had lived in these mountains and had tilled their high, misty fields since time immemorial.

"Delighted," I said.

"Please..." She gestured for us to go inside.

We laid our footwear in a neat row on the porch of the thatched farmhouse with two front doors, the place Cup-of-Tea like to call, in his diaries, *kuzu-ya*, his "Trash House." Kiku stood in its left-side entrance. One by one, barefoot, we followed her in.

Cup-of-Tea, pot-bellied and shiny-bald, lay flat on his back, snuggling a naked baby boy.

Kuro asked, "How old is the little one now?"

"Five months already," Kiku reported, beaming with pride. Then, addressing me and Kojiki, she added, "His name is Kinsaro."

My jaw dropped, the name calling to mind certain awful facts of Cup-of-Tea's biography. Kiku had already borne, and lost, three babies. This fourth, a giggling cherub with fat, red cheeks, would soon enough join his siblings in the pine-shaded graveyard. And even more heartbreaking, the lovely, heavy-lidded Kiku herself would catch pneumonia and die still quicker...in just a matter of months.

Cup-of-Tea, of course, was oblivious to these horrors that waited just around Destiny's corner. He grinned in our direction, then blew a fart sound on his delighted son's tummy. Kiku scooped up giggling Kinsaro and shuffled into an inner room. Cup-of-Tea sat up.

Kuro introduced Kojiki as a "traveling companion."

"Kojiki is it? I, too, am a beggar...Shinano Province's Chief of Beggars. Welcome!" Cup-of-Tea said.

Kojiki bowed deeply. "I thank you, sir."

Kuro introduced me next, as "a wandering priest called Mud, friend of Buck-Teeth's."

I gushed, "It's truly an honor, Master Cup-of-Tea. Truly!"

"Make yourself at home, Priest-Called-Mud. A friend of Buck-Teeth's is a friend of mine."

His warm smile drove all thoughts of predestined tragedy from my mind. I instantly felt better to the point of giddiness, though I tried hard not to show it: thrilled to be sitting by the glowing open hearth in the home of the great Cup-of-Tea. So much so, I forgot my main purpose for being there. Lucky for me, Kuro didn't. "Where's Buck-Teeth?" he asked.

"Oh, he left. About an hour ago," Cup-of-Tea answered. "You know the boy. Itchy feet."

My heart sank. "Where did he go?" I asked.

"Down to the village, first. After that, who knows?"

"But I need to talk to him...about an urgent matter." I stood. "If you'll excuse me..."

Kuro and Shiro stood too. "Stay, priest," Kuro said. "We know the village. We'll fetch him for you."

They bowed to our host, and left. The body-guard Kojiki, guarding bodies, tagged along.

"Come," Cup-of-Tea said. He led me outside to a meadow behind Trash House. He sat cross-legged in the cool shade of a great nettle tree. I sat too, across from him. The autumn afternoon was bright and breezy. Pigeons cooed in branches above; a lanky brown cow wandered and grazed.

"Master Cup-of-Tea," I said. "Your haiku mean so much to me. And I predict, someday, they'll be translated in foreign lands. Then, *you'll* be loved all over the world."

"Is that so?" Cup-of-Tea said, cleaning a toe-nail with a sliver of wood.

"Oh, I'm sure of it," I said, feeling quite pleased with this clever lead-in to my first question: "So, what advice would you give your future transla-tors?" I leaned forward and didn't breathe, eager to hear what the master had to say to one of his "future translators," me.

"But why?" he asked.

"Why what?"

"Why would people in a foreign land want my haiku? Can't they write their own?"

"Of course," I said. "But let's just suppose, in this particular foreign land, they've never heard of one-breath poetry. They'll need *your* example, Master Cup-of-Tea, to show them the way. And since they can't read the original—"

"They won't know Japanese?"

"Nope."

"Then who in that land will translate, not knowing our tongue?"

"Uh, they'll have dictionaries, tons of dictionaries," I stammered.

The cow chomped on the withered grass. A black butterfly flitted. Cup-of-Tea continued his toenail grooming.

"Well?" I asked.

"Well what?"

"Advice for the translator?" I prodded.

He sighed. "I just don't see the point."

"The point?"

"The point. Translating my words in that foreign land you talk about—why?"

"So that people can read 'em. Isn't that why you write?"

"Why does the mountain cuckoo sing?" He answered my question with a question, then closed his eyes. He lifted a hand in a "wait" gesture. Could this be what I hoped it was? Was Cup-of-Tea, in my physical presence, actually composing?

He opened his eyes and recited, slowly and surely in seventeen perfect syllables of Old Japanese: *"haikai wo... saezuru yôna... kankodori"*—which might pointlessly be translated:

like warbling
pure haiku...
mountain cuckoo

I sat in the breezy meadow behind Trash House, stunned and delighted. The haiku that Cup-of-Tea had just created was one of my all-time favorites! The wind sighed in the nettle-tree, the cow munched, a huge crow landed on the thatched roof of the nearby grain barn, cawing. Cup-of-Tea smirked at it. Then he looked over at me and chuckled. "I think they should make their own haiku, the people in that foreign land." He shooed a fly. "Are *you* from a foreign land?"

"Why do you ask?" I didn't want to lie, yet, on the other hand, didn't intend on "blowing my cover," as we spies say.

"The questions you ask. You've traveled far to come here?"

"Oh yes, Master Cup-of-Tea. Very far."

"I, too, was a wanderer. I crisscrossed the provinces. Ate my breakfast in Musashi, laid my head to rest in Kazusa. I was a drifting cloud in those days, a wind-blown spirit."

"I know," I said.

"You know?"

"Uh, I mean, I can relate. I used to walk all around too, writing haiku everywhere I went. But, recently,

I hit a dry spell. I think I was thinking about it too much, approaching it the wrong way, trying to understand and control it instead of...just letting it happen. Anyway, that's changing now. These days, on *this* trip, my haiku seem to be writing themselves again, you know?"

Cup-of-Tea smiled; he knew. His voice dropped almost to a whisper. "Who is your master?"

I hadn't given this question any thought before, but the answer popped instantly into my head and onto my lips. "Buck-Teeth."

"Buck-Teeth?"

"I first found out about haiku in the work of your student. The more I read his book, the more I liked and learned from it, till, finally, I gave it a go myself."

His smile broadened. "So young Buck-Teeth has a student already!"

"Master," I said, hoping to change the subject, "I wonder if I could ask a few more questions...about your work?"

"Why do you call it work?"

"Work, play, whatever. May I?"

"Of course."

So many questions crowded my brain, where would I begin? Some of the haiku that I was most curious about had not yet been written, so I mentally scratched those off my list. Others had been written by this point, but my questions about them touched on mere gossipy matters: the who, what, where, when...not the why. After a full minute of silent pondering, I settled on:

nightingale—
for the emperor, too
the same song

I recited it out loud, then asked, "Are *you* the nightingale?"

He looked at me blankly.

"I mean, is it autobiographical?"

I waited, but he said nothing. Perhaps he needed more examples to grasp my point. "How about this one, then?" I quoted:

chin-deep
in the fallen blossoms...
frog

Cup-of-Tea only grinned.

"Or this?" I recited:

lightning flash—
only the dog's face
is innocent

"Are all the animals in these haiku...you?" I asked.

He stood abruptly—so abruptly, I feared that I had somehow offended him. He raced across the meadow and ducked into a leaning wooden outhouse, half-buried in the drooping branches of a willow. Soon after, a burst of wild, muffled laughter emanated from within.

When he returned to our shady spot, he said nothing about my dangling question. He had, however, regained his composure—smiling calmly—so I launched a follow-up query. I recited:

borrowing an antler
the butterfly
rests

He sighed.

"I love that poem," I said. "It describes such a sweet, tender moment."

"It was that."

"But I wonder...is the butterfly symbolic? The fragile creature trustfully rests on the deer's antler, just as faithful believers must trust in the all-saving power of Amida Buddha. Is that what you meant?"

"A priestly interpretation, priest. By the way, I'm a priest, too."

"You are?"

"Priest Cup-of-Tea of Haiku Temple." He

folded his hands and bowed.

I returned the bow. "Haiku Temple. Is that a real place?"

"You should know. You're a member."

"Really? Where is it, Master Cup-of-Tea? Can we go there?"

But before he could answer, Kuro, Shiro and Kojiki came trotting up the path from the village. One by one, they plopped to their knees in the grass.

"Bad news," Kuro said, gasping for breath. "Buck-Teeth's vanished!"

* * *

"He never stays long," Cup-of-Tea said, then added warmly, "The boy's a drifting cloud."

"Did he tell anyone in the village where he's drifting to this time?" I asked, but Kuro, Shiro and Kojiki all shook their heads, *no*.

"What direction did he go, then? Did someone at least see that?"

"South," Kuro said. "But that's not much of a clue. Half of Japan lies that way."

"Then that's the half I'll check." I stood. I wished I could have stayed and chatted more with Cup-of-Tea; I was especially curious about the "Haiku

Temple" he had just mentioned. But I had written myself into Old Japan expressly to interview Buck-Teeth, and with each passing minute his trail was growing colder. "I'm going south," I announced.

"Now?" Kuro asked incredulously.

"Yes."

"Before dinner?" He frowned.

"You're most welcome to stay and eat," Cup-of-Tea said. "I can smell Kiku's cooking."

"Thanks, but no, Master Cup-of-Tea. I must find Buck-Teeth!" I bowed to the great teacher, then asked his disciples, Kuro and Shiro, "Would you like to come with me?"

But before Shiro could gesture his response, Kuro said, emphatically, "No!"

Shiro frowned.

"Well, I must be off," I said. I bade farewell to all, apologized for my haste, and started down the hill. When I reached the tiny village below, I heard heavy footsteps stomping behind me. I turned and saw Kojiki.

"The one in white wants me to go with you," he said.

"But the ninja tried to kill *them*, not me. *They* need you!"

Kojiki shrugged. "He insisted. He gave me a look I couldn't refuse. And this." He held up a leather pouch and shook it, jingling coins. "I'm guarding *you*, now."

"I just hope they're safe," I muttered.

"I can't be two places at once, can I?"

* * *

I can. Unlike Kojiki, who lives and breathes only in Old Japan, I live and breathe there *and* here, at my little table in my upstairs shotgun apartment in New Orleans...hunched over blue ink-scribbled pages inside which the "there" and the "here" co-exist.

Being there and here is a curious thing. I'm the "author" who just now took a gulp of muddy, hot coffee and glanced out the window at a low, over-cast Louisiana sky. But I'm also the saffron-robed traveler in Old Japan, who at this moment happens to be entering the great, red gate of Zenkô Temple with Kojiki at his side. Of these simultaneous ex-istences, the one in Japan feels, I confess, a bit more real. I smell incense smoldering as I stroll past vendors on the long, wide promenade between Zenkôji's red gate and its matching main hall. En route to the latter I pause at a *juzu* stand, consid-ering whether or not to purchase a Buddhist ro-sary. After all, I *am* a priest. I admire a particularly fine loop of brown, hand-carved wooden beads, but then remember that I have no money. I won't ask Kojiki to buy me this with his bodyguard's pay. So I set the *juzu* down on the little table, clickety-click. The old woman regards me with large, disappointed eyes.

This is *real* to me. But my other life, the one that requires me now to go to the kitchen counter for a refill, feels... Just a second.

I'm back. The coffee's strong and black. Last night I dropped a pickle jar. I swept up all the pieces, I *thought*, but just now caught a sliver of glass in my heel. I've pulled it out and tossed it in the trash. It hurts, and yet, even so, this so-called "real" life of mine seems queerly remote and insignificant compared to the much "realer" reality of that dim, cool temple, long ago, in Old Japan.

* * *

"We should ask the priests about your friend," Kojiki broke my reverie. "Most travelers in these mountains stop here. *He* might have."

"I hope so," I said. It was our second day in pursuit of the elusive "drifting cloud," Buck-Teeth, and our pace had been relentless. I hoped that we were gaining on him.

We approached the main temple hall. Kojiki

kicked off his clogs, I my Reeboks. We stepped into the dim, cool foyer.

"There's one," Kojiki whispered, nodding.

A young monk was sweeping the floor with a straw broom.

"Excuse me—"

"Careful!" he warned. "There's a broken pot over here. The pieces are sharp."

We stopped at a safe distance. "We're looking for a traveler, a poet who goes by the name of Buck-Teeth," I said.

"Ah, Buck-Teeth." The monk nodded his smooth-shaved head. "I know him."

"Has he been here recently? We think he might have come this way."

The monk swept porcelain shards, dirt, and the remnants of some sort of flowering plant into a neat pile. "He spent the night, last night. But he left."

"Did he say where he was going?" I asked, breathless with excitement.

"Oh yes."

"That's great! Where?"

"To a place he calls 'Morning-glory Mansion'."

"I've heard of it!" I exclaimed. "That's his hermitage!" I was ecstatic. My search would soon be over! I would quickly visit Buck-Teeth at his famous hut, and he'd clear up for me, at long last, the historical enigma of the four-and-a-half-month gap in his journal.

"And where, exactly, is Morning-glory Mansion?" I was eager to snap into place the final piece of the jigsaw puzzle I had come all the way to Old Japan to complete.

The acolyte shrugged. "He didn't say."

"But *you* must know! I mean, Morning-glory Mansion's famous, isn't it?"

"Famous?" His look was blank.

I sighed. "Shit." I had miscalculated. Buck-Teeth was way more famous in future time than in his own—a common problem among poets.

"He did say something, though," he added.

Hope rekindled in my heart, but a bucket of cold water soon came sloshing down to douse it.

"It's on a mountain."

"Oh swell," Kojiki groaned. "*That* narrows it down!"

RED HERRING

ANOTHER THURSDAY AFTERNOON, another gathering of writers in a corner office on a little college campus deep in the Deep South...

"Why did you caricature Nakamura?" Micky was first to speak after I distributed copies of, and finished reading out loud, my latest installment. My muse, the Buddha, has been pushing my pen so fast and furiously these days, my writing group lags far behind the current point in the book. As of that particular Thursday, they had only just reached the end of Chapter Two, in which I describe my strange interview with Professor Nakamura.

"You think I caricatured him?" I asked.

"I should say so! You have him acting like some kind of paranoid idiot." Micky eased back in her big wooden rocking chair, her gray eyes flashing with challenge.

I didn't know what to say. Micky, our English

Department's deconstructionist for whom texts have no "totality," no central meaning—was concerned with the truthfulness of my portrayal of a character? *Very* odd!

"It hardly seems appropriate. In fact, it's libelous," she added.

"But I changed his name."

"You *barely* changed his name. Everyone who knows him will know right away who you're talking about."

"Do *you* know him, Micky?"

Her eyes dropped to the pile of photocopied pages in her lap. "We've, uh, met...at conferences. Last year, we co-chaired a panel. I find him to be a spectacular intellect, gentle, kind—"

"So what?" Chaz from Arkansas interrupted, his brown hair shaggy-long, a tiny silver sword dangling from an ear. "Dave's writing fiction here. Why not make his professor a bit kooky? I like him that way."

"So do I." Soft-spoken Paul, the newest addition to our weekly writers' group, stroked his sandy-red beard. "But Nakamura's behavior does raise certain questions. Will we, as readers, discover why he acted so curiously? I mean, I'd hate to see him turn out a red herring."

Micky jumped back in. "Red herring or not, he deserves at least a modicum of respect!"

"But I *do* respect him, Micky. I bought his book, didn't I? And who did I turn to when I needed advice? He's *the* authority on Buck-Teeth. But when he kicked me out of his office..."

I paused, my own words echoing in my head. Nakamura was *the* authority on Buck-Teeth. *The* authority...

"He knows!" I blurted. "He *must* know!"

"Knows what?" Paul asked.

"Morning-glory Mansion!"

"What are you yammering about?" Chaz wondered.

"Buck-Teeth's hermitage! Nakamura must know where it is."

"Even so, he doesn't seem to want to talk to you," Paul observed.

"Maybe he won't have to," I said. "You see, there's a map..."

* * *

"I'M HERE about the mouse," I announced.

"Mouse?" The secretary arched her thin, drawn-on eyebrows. "What mouse?"

I reached into a plastic Winn Dixie bag and pulled out a computer mouse by its long, modular tail. "It's for Professor Nakamura. If you let me in his office, I'll pop this puppy on and be on my way."

"I didn't know he was having computer problems."

"Mouse," I corrected her. "He's having mouse problems."

"Do I know you?" Her eyes narrowed suspiciously.

I had anticipated my being remembered from my first visit, so I launched into the cover story I had prepared. "I stopped by a month or so ago. His hard drive was acting up."

"So you're from Tech Support?"

"Can I get started?"

The good professor, I knew, was at lunch. I had staked out his building all morning, skipping my own classes at my smaller, less prestigious university. When he finally exited the front door in his dark, tailored suit, I had scampered around to a side entrance, up a flight of stairs, into small reception area labeled, "Asian Languages and Literatures." There I now stood, swinging my mouse like a hypnotist's pendulum.

"Well, I suppose it's all right." The secretary, short and round, fished a key ring from a drawer and led me down a carpeted hall to Nakamura's inner sanctum. She unlocked its door and opened it.

"This won't take long." I stepped into the room and behind the desk, switching on the black computer. The only other object on the desktop was a clear glass vase, today's selection a red carnation. The machine booted up with a flurry of clicks and pings. The secretary left me alone.

My plan was working splendidly, but I had to move fast. I wheeled about-face and examined the true object of my visit: the great, green wall map of Japan behind the professor's desk. His tiny, red-inked notes amassed in three areas: Kyoto, the emperor's capital; Tokyo, the Shogun's city formerly called Edo; and, far to the west, bumpy with mountains, Nagano Prefecture, Old Japan's Shinano Province...Buck-Teeth's and Cup-of-Tea's home turf. I focused on this last section, poring over it in search of Morning-glory Mansion.

The professor's annotations were all done in small, crabbed and, to me, mostly incomprehensible Japanese. But I had memorized one important *kanji* before coming here: *iori*, which means, in English, a hut or hermitage. And soon enough, I found one!

I committed the spot to memory. It wasn't far from my current location in Old Japan, as the crow flies: follow the river to where it forks, cross it, then head due east, over the first mountain. Halfway up the second mountain...*iori*.

I just hoped it was the right *iori*!

* * *

Kojiki sounded suspicious. "You suddenly know the way?"

"I can't explain it," I said. We had reached the bank of the rushing, white waters of Chikuma River. A wooden footbridge with as many planks missing as present sagged over the torrent. "We cross here." I pointed east across the river at a misty, blue hulk of mountain. "Morning-glory Mansion's on the other side of *that.*"

"Are you sure, priest? Climbing that thing's not going to be easy."

"I'm positive," I said, mentally crossing my fingers.

I started across the swaying bridge, avoiding gaps, eager to find the elusive Buck-Teeth. Kojiki scurried behind me. Soon, we reached the other side and stepped into the cool, dark shade of an ancient cedar forest, its colossal trees with Volkswagen-sized trunks, their tops lost in the clouds. We started up a path.

Suddenly, a high-pitched whistle. Kojiki's left hand, fingers splayed wide, flew in front of my face.

"Wha—?" Why had he so rudely blocked my vision, and what was that odd sound, that *thunk*? My eyes pulled focus to his hand and to a thing protruding from the back of it: a thin steel blade gleaming with blood.

"Get down!" he hissed, pushing me to the

ground with his right hand. As he did so, the left one turned, revealing the small black hilt of a dagger that, had he not snagged it from the air with his own flesh, would have nailed me between the eyes.

"It's him!" the bodyguard whispered. "I saw him."

"Who? The ninja?"

But before he could reply, a cold, stern voice shouted from the shadowy depths of the woods, "That was a cute stunt, invading my office!"

At first I didn't believe my ears. The strangely familiar voice had addressed me in perfect English! And then I knew who it was, who it had to be, though the truth was beyond baffling.

Professor Nakamura! What was *he* doing in Old Japan?

PART TWO

BUCK-TEETH

We hiked up and over the mountain, watching for the ninja who, we feared, was watching us. The hole in Kojiki's hand oozed, but no tendons had been cut; he could wiggle all his fingers. After washing it in the river and wrapping his hand with a strip of cloth torn from his ragged robe, the beggar-bodyguard stashed Nakamura's dagger in his satchel. "I may return it to its owner one day," he muttered grimly.

Though we both sensed the ninja's eyes upon us, no additional knives came flying from the shadows. We slept in shifts under the stars, taking turns keeping watch, and the next morning at daybreak hiked down a winding, mossy path into a deep valley clotted with clouds. If the "hermitage" marked on Professor Nakamura's office map belonged to Buck-Teeth, as I hoped it did, the young haiku poet with the famous overbite awaited us somewhere just ahead.

"It's not far now...I think," I said.

"You just *think*?"

"No. I'm sure of it. Morning-glory Mansion is...up there." I pointed at the steep forest that loomed ahead, ghostly, in the haze.

Kojiki sighed. "I hope you're right, priest."

We found a path and followed it all morning, zigzagging up through the cloud-scraping cedars. The mist gradually burned away, and the noon sun dappled the damp, spongy path with crazy hieroglyphs of light. I contemplated writing a haiku about that path, that light, and our soft footfalls on both, but fear stopped me. I felt certain, somehow, that Nakamura the ninja slunk in the shadows nearby, holding me and Kojiki in his cold, calculating gaze.

"Look!" Kojiki pointed. Tendrils of gray smoke rose in the forest ahead. We hiked in that direction and soon found a campfire near a dilapidated hut almost completely buried in vines. Next to that fire, in front of that hut, dangling a smoke-blackened kettle from a knobby bamboo walking stick...sat Buck-Teeth!

"Good day." He nodded his head politely.

"Good day!" Kojiki and I replied.

"It's so good to see you, Buck-Teeth," I said. "Allow me to introduce my companion, Kojiki."

Buck-Teeth and Kojiki exchanged bows.

"Please, sit," Buck-Teeth said. "The tea should be ready soon, if you don't mind sharing a cup." As he spoke, he revealed the front teeth that had earned for him the cruel childhood nickname that he later had embraced, defiantly, as his haiku name. In reality, they jutted out just slightly. Modern orthodontics could have easily corrected this minor flaw in Buck-Teeth's bashful smile.

He filled a chipped earthenware cup with steaming green liquid and handed it to me, saying, "Please."

"Thanks," I said. I took a sip.

"Don't I know you, priest?" Buck-Teeth studied my face intently.

"Aren't you two friends?" Kojiki asked in a puzzled tone.

"I, uh, wasn't completely honest with you, Kojiki," I stammered. "You see, actually, I know Buck-Teeth...but he doesn't know me."

"Yet I could almost swear, priest, that I do," Buck-Teeth said.

"I don't see how. I know you only through your writing, Buck-Teeth. I've admired it for years. And I'm grateful. It was your haiku that introduced me to one-breath poetry—and to the work of your master, Cup-of-Tea. I thank you for that. My name, by the way, is Mud." I bowed.

Buck-Teeth's smile faded. His shoulders

slumped and his eyes grew sad. It was true what they said about him: he wore his heart on his sleeve, his emotion from moment to moment easily readable in his open-book face.

"What is it?" I asked. "Did I offend you?"

He shook his head slowly. "No. But hearing you talk about haiku like that...it's just too bad that it's over. You see, it died."

Kojiki frowned. "Died?"

"Yes," Buck-Teeth said. "I'm through with haiku."

"But why, Buck-Teeth? Why have you quit haiku?" I posed the urgent question that had inspired my deep-cover mission to Old Japan. Holding my breath, I awaited Buck-Teeth's answer.

But he didn't answer. Instead, he said quietly, "I'll show you."

He ducked into his hut and reemerged with the hefty diary that one day would become a priceless literary treasure. He opened its delicate, rice-paper pages to his last entry and recited:

she cools her sunburnt
face...
moon

"That's it. The end. The very end." He solemnly closed the book.

I waited, expecting more, but Buck-Teeth said

nothing.

I shrugged. "I don't get it. Why, Buck-Teeth? Why should that haiku be the end?"

"Don't you see?" He held up the diary. "It's a graveyard. Everything in it, flat, dead!" He tossed the book back into the darkness of the hut, where it landed with a thump.

"That's a damn shame," Kojiki said. "But I understand. I, too, have gone through career changes. I was an actor, once. Perhaps you saw me in Edo?"

"I don't get to the big city much," Buck-Teeth said.

"Why do you say haiku is dead?" I asked.

"It just is."

Seeing that I was getting nowhere with this topic, I quickly brought up a more pressing, life-or-death one. "Kojiki here is my bodyguard, Buck-Teeth," I said. "You see, a ninja has been following us. You haven't seen one lurking about, have you?"

"No," Buck-Teeth said.

"He attacked your friends, Shiro and Kuro."

Buck-Teeth gasped. "Are they all right?"

"Yes, praise Buddha. And he tried to kill me yesterday, but Kojiki saved me. I don't want to alarm you...but *you* might be in danger too."

"Me?"

I nodded. "His mind's twisted, Buck-Teeth. He studies poetry. He studies poets. But, it seems, he wants to kill them."

"But I'm not a poet anymore!"

"Still, you should come with us. Let's leave this place!"

Buck-Teeth looked down into the dying flames, his easy-to-read face ashen and defeated. "I don't care what happens to me," he muttered.

* * *

CUP-OF-TEA belonged to the True Teaching Pure Land sect of Shinran, the Buddhist master who recommended that we trust in a saving power beyond the ego. Shinran named that power Amida Buddha; the ancient Chinese named it Tao; Christians name it Amazing Grace.

Though Cup-of-Tea was evasive on this point when I interviewed him, I'm still convinced that his poetry is filled with Buddhist parables, as in this example:

a flea jumps
in the laughing Buddha's
mouth

On the literal level, the mouth of a wooden or bronze Buddha receives an errant, hopping flea.

To be sure, the flea didn't consciously aim to land in the maw of the Great Compassionate One. However, the fact that it has "randomly" done so is a happy reminder of a benevolent power at work in the universe. In that power, Shinran advised, we should devoutly, utterly trust.

Trust is important in haiku writing, too. The poet must trust in the moment and let the right words spout. A haiku can't be forced any more than a Buddhist can force Amida, or a Christian can force Jesus, to save him or her.

If one pridefully declares, "*I* write my haiku; *I* take credit!" the well of poetry dries up.

Might this be what happened to Buck-Teeth on the night of the harvest moon eclipse? I decided to ask him.

* * *

He stood at the dark entrance of his vine-covered hut. He made no move to come with me and Kojiki. I worried that even now Professor Nakamura might be aiming some razor-sharp ninja weapon at any or all of us. With a sinking feeling that time was running out, I blurted, "Tell me, Buck-Teeth, what happened that night? Did you find yourself forcing words? Did ego get in the way?"

He stared at me intently. I thought he was formulating a response, but instead: "I've got it! It was in a dream I saw you. A dream, priest!"

"Really?"

"Yes. A strange dream...years ago. I dreamed I was in a foreign place but somehow could speak the language. There was a crowded street with taverns everywhere I looked...it was a bright, moonlit night. I seem to remember writing some haiku there, but with some sort of odd cylinder that looked nothing like a brush. And young women—beautiful women—bared their bodies in the taverns. This, I remember, was the dream's main topic. But before it ended, I caught sight of *you*, priest, through a large window. You sat among the revelers. It was definitely you!"

I grinned. So Buck-Teeth assumed that his visit to Bourbon Street, described in my first book, had been just a dream!

"And then what happened?" I prodded.

"Then...I woke up."

He seemed so profoundly amazed to have met—in the flesh—me, a figment of a long-ago dream, I decided to use this fact to my advantage.

"That dream was a premonition, Buck-Teeth. It means I've been sent to you...by the Buddha. You must trust in the Buddha's power. Come with me. Let's get off this mountain before the ninja strikes!"

"He's right." Kojiki nodded gravely. "If you saw the priest in a dream, it means something."

"Will you come with us?" I asked.

Buck-Teeth sighed. "I suppose."

"Great!" I could hardly wait to get away from Morning-glory Mansion. I imagined the dagger-tossing assassin behind every bush and tree trunk.

Buck-Teeth packed his travel satchel, leaned his hut's bramble door against the entrance, kicked dirt on his little, dying fire. He picked up his walking stick. "I'm ready."

"Aren't you forgetting something?" I asked.

He looked at me blankly.

"Your diary! You're not taking it?"

"No need for that."

"Get it! You'll need it someday, I promise."

"I told you. Haiku died."

"Well, bring it anyway. Humor me. Remember, I'm here to help, as predicted by your dream."

He wavered. "I didn't mention this before because I didn't want to offend you. But, in that dream, when I saw you...I felt something."

"Really? What did you feel, Buck-Teeth, in that dream of yours?"

"Hate," he said, looking down at dirt and ashes. "I hated you, priest."

THE BOX

BUCK-TEETH'S DREAMED HATRED of me didn't prevent him from leaving Morning-glory Mansion in my company, his diary tucked in his well-worn satchel. I was glad. With a murderous ninja afoot, I figured there was safety in numbers. And besides, I hoped to learn from Buck-Teeth why haiku had "died" for him. Perhaps I could help him to recover his poetic voice. This had to be done, I figured, by New Year's Day at the very latest, the time of his next fated entry in the diary.

"What's the date today?" I asked.

"Ninth Month, Third Day," Kojiki said.

"Good."

It *seemed* like plenty of time, but Nakamura's presence in the book complicated matters. Could he change destiny? Could he alter what *should* happen? So far, he had attacked two poets...and me. Was Buck-Teeth, too, in danger? Was his haiku legacy in jeopardy? This thought was especially disturbing. If the ninja killed Buck-Teeth, posterity would be robbed of one of its most beloved poets. The Puffin Corporation would never commission its fine though flawed translation of his diary, which means that I would never stumble upon a copy of said translation at a sidewalk sale in the French Quarter one glorious Saturday morning in March, never learn about one-breath poetry, never become a haiku translator and dabbler. Not only Buck-Teeth's, but my own literary existence was at stake!

I kept these dark thoughts to myself. Buck-Teeth was visibly on edge, hiking on the Shogun's highway with a phantom priest that he had dreamed about and despised. And Kojiki's eyes shifted up and down, side to side, anxiously watching for the watcher.

"Writing's a dangerous thing," I muttered.

"What's that, priest?" Kojiki asked.

"Nothing. How far to the next town? I'm starved."

"Tobu village is about a *ri* from here," Kojiki answered. "But we'll have to beg a bit. The money's gone."

"Already?" My stomach grumbled and growled; I wasn't about to deny it the pleasure of large portions of fine Old Japanese cuisine. And so, rounding a curve...

"Look!" I pointed at a clump of weeds in the roadside ditch.

"What is it, priest?" Kojiki asked.

"Down there. I think I see something."

Kojiki squatted, his eyes tracking in the direction I pointed. Then he saw it too: a glossy brown object.

He jumped down into the ditch to investigate.

"It's a box!" he reported.

"Open it!"

He did so...and gasped.

Buck-Teeth, who had trudged all afternoon in tense silence, asked, "What is it?"

Tears shimmered in Kojiki's eyes. He looked up from the bottom of the weedy ditch, stunned and speechless. When he finally did speak, his voice was trembling. "Never in my life," he said, "have I seen so many coins!"

We were rich.

* * *

IN JAPAN there's no such thing as "finders keepers." I learned this lesson the summer I visited there. I was strolling through the bustling underground mall of Ikebukuro Station in Tokyo, when I spotted a crisp, new bank bill lying seductively on the gleaming, polished floor. But before I could grab it, a little old lady approached from the opposite direction and scooped it up. And then, incredibly, she waved over a passing cop and handed it...to him!

Later, a Japanese friend explained that what I had witnessed had been the norm. When most folks find cash in Japan, most folks turn it in at the nearest police box. If they lose cash, they go to the nearest police box, and nine times out of ten, they get it back.

Amazing.

Growing up in the U.S.A., I naturally would have snatched that moolah and tucked it in my pocket, had I beaten the old lady to it. Finder's keepers.

I was reminded of the incident in the Ikebukuro station as I now faced off with Buck-Teeth and Kojiki, clashing culturally with them over the issue of found money.

"Of *course* we can keep it," I insisted.

"But it belongs to somebody," Buck-Teeth said. "A rich person. A daimyo, perhaps."

Kojiki, who up to this point had seemed thrilled by our discovery, now frowned. "It could mean big trouble, taking a daimyo's money."

"We should give it to the authorities," Buck-Teeth added, piously.

But my stomach growled even louder; I was *very*

hungry.

And so, with a few swift strokes of the pen my other self at the little kitchen table in New Orleans, peering into this ancient world that I had entered as a spy, subtly altered the scene, writing in a crucial difference...

* * *

"There's a note!" Kojiki exclaimed after prying open the lacquered wood strongbox.

"What does it say?" I asked.

"It says, 'To whomever finds this money, keep it. Use it well. I am a merchant who has squandered his life concerned only with accounts and profits. Now an old man, I turn to the Buddha and thoughts of the Pure Land. I relinquish all the trifling wealth of this dewdrop world, *Namu Amida Butsu'!*"

We split the loot three ways. Kojiki's and Buck-Teeth's satchels bulged with coins. I carried my share in the shiny box the money had come in. I was famished and eager to feast.

And feast we did. At the village of Tobu we dined in style. The innkeeper at first looked skeptical when we ordered several courses of high-country delicacies. But Kojiki opened his hand and dropped a pile of fresh-minted coins on the table.

From that point on, it was the royal treatment for us. The innkeeper's wife and three daughters busied themselves late into the evening, preparing and rushing to our table tray after tray of Old Japanese munchies: spicy pond-snails, roasted pheasant, raw horse, and the thin-sliced strips of boiled beef they call *shabu-shabu*. All the while we partook of round after round of high-grade rice wine, which I was liking more than I would have thought possible, that first morning I sniffed the stuff on Inacho's verandah.

Kojiki belched profoundly and lifted his cup. "To our good fortune!"

"*Kampai!*" We downed our sake in a gulp, samurai-style, even sullen Buck-Teeth.

"So, priest," Kojiki said. "Now that you're rich beyond a miser's dream, what plans have you?"

"Well, I haven't given it much thought," I replied. "*This* is nice, though. I wouldn't mind eating this good every chance I get."

He smirked. "You're strange, priest. No qualms? No worry about the burden of wealth sinking you in a sea of desire—all that priestly mumbo jumbo? Because, if you fear the karmic danger of your share, I'd be more than happy to take it off your hands."

"Thanks, but no," I said, grinning.

Kojiki grinned back. "Devil!"

"I'm giving *my* share to Mother," Buck-Teeth, who had brooded silently all through our feast, commented. "She's slaved in the fields her whole life. She deserves a bit of comfort. I wasn't there to help her, all those years I wasted on poetry."

His eyes were red and distant.

"More sake!" Kojiki shouted. One of the innkeeper's daughters rushed over to refill our cups.

"How about you, Kojiki? What are your plans?" I asked.

"My plans? I'm going straight to Edo and buy me the best damn armor a samurai ever wore. And two swords of the finest steel. And a proper war-horse. No, make that three horses. I don't want my friends to have to walk!"

"Thank you." I bowed.

"I thank you, too." Buck-Teeth bowed also. "But I prefer walking."

"As you wish," Kojiki said. "And after that bit of shopping, I'll visit Yoshiwara in style."

This piqued my interest. I had read about the Shogun's fabulous brothel district on the outskirts of Edo: a walled-in pleasure town filled with thousands of courtesans.

"May I tag along?" I asked.

"Why not? Yes. Come, priest, if you think your karma can stand it. And I want you to know, though

I'm rich now, I still intend on protecting you as long as you like."

"I'm honored," I said, bowing again.

Buck-Teeth excused himself and stumbled off to his bath with shoulders slumped, head hanging low.

"That boy needs to loosen up," Kojiki sniffed.

MUDA

NOW THAT HAIKU WAS DEAD for him, Buck-Teeth believed that all his years spent writing it had been *muda*, a Japanese word that means "wasted," "stupid," "in vain." Coincidentally, his master, Cup-of-Tea, uses this word in several poems:

vain clouds
forming vain peaks
in vain

in vain
the baby bird begs...
a stepchild

moon! blossoms!
49 years walking around
a waste

Muda denotes useless effort. Summer clouds billow to fantastic, unreal peaks one after another—

but for what? Their atmospheric grand performance accomplishes nothing that abides. In the second example, "stepchild" is a euphemism for "motherless." The baby bird yawns for a worm, but being a "stepchild" [as Cup-of-Tea was], its pitiful gesture is essentially *muda*...useless. And in the third haiku, Cup-of-Tea summarizes his forty-nine years spent wandering and babbling poetry about autumn's moon and spring's blossoms—as a fabulous waste.

Viewed together, these haiku speak volumes about the master's understanding of poetry in the great scheme of things: it's vain as a cloud-mountain, useless as an abandoned fledgling's cry, not likely to win anyone the worm of reward. And yet, though he felt this way about his art, Cup-of-Tea kept on writing.

Why, then, did his protégé, Buck-Teeth, realizing this same truth about haiku, quit?

My first night as a millionaire in Old Japan, I lay awake for hours in my eighteen-and-a-half-tatami mat suite, pondering this dilemma. Near midnight, I came up with an excellent [I thought] plan. Tomorrow morning, I would remind Buck-Teeth that Cup-of-Tea continued to write despite haiku's uselessness, or perhaps even because of it. The master's example, I hoped, would light the way for his befuddled student.

Lying spread-eagle on my futon, my belly pleasantly full, I was confident that all would be well. Buck-Teeth would listen to me, heed the example of Cup-of-Tea, and once again pick up his writing brush. Feeling clever, drowsy and drunk, to happy dreams I drifted.

WORDS

"Yesterday, Buck-Teeth, you described haiku as a 'waste'. And you're right. Poetry *is* useless, as far as the workaday world goes. It doesn't grow rice. It doesn't catch a fish. Even Master Cup-of-Tea regards it as an insubstantial thing, fleeting as a cloud-mountain and as worthless, in the material sense, as an orphan bird's cheep. And yet, still he writes. So why don't you?"

Buck-Teeth, Kojiki, and I strolled under a white autumn sky. Wind whistled over the mountains, sighed in the fathomless cedars. It was cool, brisk weather, perfect for tramping on the Shogun's highway that snaked its liesurely way east toward the Shogun's great city, Edo.

"You're right, priest," Buck-Teeth said, clacking the road with his walking stick. "My master taught me, by example more than words, that haiku is play, not the serious work of the world of man. But ordinary folk don't understand how one can devote one's life to playtime. Like my father. He approved of my haiku training only because he thought I might profit by it. And I nearly did. Lord Kaga wanted me in his retinue at one point. I would have had prestige, security...and my father's pride in me."

"What happened?" Kojiki asked.

"I walked away."

"I know, Buck-Teeth," I said, then hastened to add, "I mean, I've heard of that. And I've always admired you for your dedication to your art. When success and approval threatened it, you wandered into the mountains. That was a wonderful thing."

Buck-Teeth said nothing, striking his stick a bit harder on the hard-packed dirt.

I continued. "But haiku's uselessness shouldn't kill it. Look at Cup-of-Tea! So I ask you again: Why did it 'die' for you, the night of the eclipse?"

"You're a curious one, Priest Mud." Buck-Teeth smiled sadly. "And I'd love to answer your question, if only I could. All that I'm sure of, though, is that something happened that night. Like a lantern snuffed by an icy wind. I was talking to a stranger—"

"A stranger? Who?"

"If I knew his name, I wouldn't call him a stranger," Buck-Teeth answered petulantly. "He came late to Inacho's party but didn't drink a drop. And as the moon darkened, he began lecturing loudly, claiming that the moon wasn't at all sick, as the old people said...that it was only a case of the earth's shadow crossing it. Nothing mystical, nothing magical. Master Cup-of-Tea clucked his tongue; he disapproved of this know-it-all stranger. And then, the stranger sat next to me, just inches away, though I could hardly see him in those dark clothes."

"Dark clothes?" Kojiki narrowed his eyes.

I was suspicious, too. "Could he have been a ninja?"

"I *assumed* he was a poet. He said all sorts of things about haiku, about the master's, Kuro's, and my own writing. He knew so many details."

"What kind of details?" I asked with a sinking feeling.

"Like what we wrote, when we wrote it, where we were, who we were with. He seemed to know more about our poetry than we did. It was entertaining at first, a dazzling display. But the more the dark stranger spoke, the more uneasy I felt."

"What else did he say?"

"It wasn't so much 'what' but 'how'. He spoke of haiku as a thing to be...dissected. Like my poem of the evening, the one I read to you...my last. He went on and on about its structure, its season word, its cutting word...by the time he finished I felt like he'd pulled the wings off a butterfly, exposing the ugly, fidgeting bug at its core. It was horrible because he was right. My haiku was that fidgeting bug. And then, suddenly, it stopped fidgeting. It lay on the page, dead and cold. The moon returned, but I felt no joy in it."

"The bastard," I muttered.

"Don't say that! I'm grateful to the stranger. He opened my eyes! But I can't answer your question, priest. I don't know why haiku died for me that night; I just know that it did, the moment I saw it for what it really is: seventeen hollow sounds in a five-seven-five pattern with a season word, a cutting word...in other words, words. Just words. That's all it is. All it ever was. All it *can* be. What life can words have?" He slammed his stick down, hard.

"If you think about it," Kojiki said gently, "no life at all. But perhaps that's the problem. You're thinking too much!"

Buck-Teeth shrugged his shoulders. "I can't un-know what I know."

ANTICIPATION

DAYS PASSED.

We drew closer to Edo, the Shogun's bustling city. I could hardly wait to squander my newfound wealth in the pleasure district of Yoshiwara. My recent frustration with Hasuko the tea-girl heightened my erotic anticipation. As we trudged along, I pictured myself lounging in some sumptuous brothel, being serviced by Old Japan's most ravishing beauties.

"How far is it?" I asked.

"You're an impatient priest, aren't you?" Kojiki smiled wolfishly. "But to answer your question, we'll be in Edo by this afternoon."

"Shall we stop and see if Kuro made it home safely?" Buck-Teeth asked. "It's on the way."

"Fine by me," Kojiki said.

I wasn't thrilled with the prospect of delaying debauchery for the sake of a social call, but in the spirit of Japanese self-sacrifice for the good of the group, I grunted my assent.

We walked along for a while, their sandals and my Reeboks slapping the road.

"That was a terrible thing he did, Buck-Teeth," I commented.

"Who?" Buck-Teeth asked.

"That stranger. The one who killed haiku for you."

"He's not to blame, priest. He only showed me the truth. That's no crime."

"I agree," Kojiki said. "But artists don't trade in truth. Trust me, Buck-Teeth; I know. In my acting career I practiced the art of pretending. Lust, terror, rage...I killed and I died—countless times. And none of it was true, but it *seemed* true, both to me and to my audience. Perhaps—"

Kojiki froze.

"Perhaps what?" Buck-Teeth asked.

"Shhh." The bodyguard's eyes shifted wildly in all directions.

Then I noticed that the birds had stopped singing.

"He's back," Kojiki whispered. "Everyone, get down!"

* * *

Lady Plum glided through the icy palace. From room to room, in a blood-red kimono, she moved quickly, quietly on bare feet.

On the verandah she found Takako, her lily-pale lady-in-waiting, waiting.

"Back so soon?" Takako stood, stifling a yawn.

"He's finished with me...for now."

"I'll summon the palanquin, then." Takako slipped on her wooden clogs and hurried across the dark courtyard to wake the bearers. The click-clack, click-clack of her footsteps sounded terribly loud to Lady Plum. "The girl must learn to tread more daintily," she whispered to the shadows.

The shadows whispered back, "I agree."

"Who's there?!" She yanked from her mass of piled-up hair a dagger-sharp pin. "Takako?"

But it couldn't have been the girl; she had click-clacked away into the night. The voice that had spoken just now had been close, very close, and so... cold. She turned a slow circle, glaring at the shadows, ready to jab.

"I won't hurt you," the voice said.

She wheeled around and gasped. A ninja emerged from the darkest corner of the verandah.

"I'm protected by the Shogun! If I scream, a hundred samurai come running!"

The masked man nodded. "I know. But I assure

you, lady, I'm here for your own good."

The click-clack of Takako's clogs sounded now like a blessing to Lady Plum. The girl was returning, followed by four brawny servants shouldering the poles of a palanquin.

"I have a proposition for you," the ninja whispered. "The details are spelled out here." He handed her a slip of rice paper. "I'll be in touch." He melted back into blackness.

The red palanquin was lowered to the ground. Takako opened its little sliding door and Lady Plum crawled in, trembling, clutching the ninja's note.

* * *

CROWS CAWED in barren, yellow fields. Cicadas chirred. A farm dog barked. Kojiki sighed, relieved to hear these normal sounds resume.

Though he had quit being a samurai years ago, Kojiki's military instincts were superb. He had accurately sensed the ninja's proximity, though this proximity wasn't exactly physical. Somehow, his warrior radar had detected Nakamura lurking in an adjacent page of this book that envelops us. Another page turned, and the danger passed.

"He's gone," Kojiki announced.

"Who's gone?" Buck-Teeth asked.

"That ninja we've been telling you about," Kojiki said. "He came close just now. Very close. But he chose not to show himself...this time."

"What does he want?" Buck-Teeth's eyes widened, his easy-to-read face blanching with fear.

"He wants to kill us, Buck-Teeth," I said. "He wants to kill haiku."

FROM KURO'S DIARY

Ninth Month. 24th Day. Cloudy.

All things, great and small, fade in this dew-drop world. Even in my morning tea, tragedy…

dead by drowning
in the deep cup
gnat

Buck-Teeth arrived today, accompanied by Priest Mud and the beggar samurai whom we know as Kojiki. Right away I detected a strange, quiet sorrow in Buck-Teeth's eyes. First chance I got, I pulled him aside and asked, "What's wrong?"

"What do you mean?"

"I know you. Something's the matter, Buck-Teeth. So tell me, what?"

He sighed. "It would be easier to say what's right."

"It's not that geisha again, the one in the cherry-blossom kimono?" I asked.

He sighed. "No, not her, Kuro. I haven't seen her since the day she vanished...years ago."

"Then what?" I asked. "You look so glum."

"If I look glum, it's because I've come around to *your* way of thinking."

"My way of thinking?"

"Kuro, you always say that nothing lasts, that nothing permanently matters. Now, I finally understand you. I agree with you. All is *mujô*: fading to nothingness so quickly, it's pointless to cling to anything, even to haiku. *Especially* to haiku."

I smiled, proud of the boy. At last his eyes were open!

"Good work, Buck-Teeth," I said, clapping him on the back. "After dinner, let's take a walk, you and I. This will be a fine evening for haiku. We'll write about all the foolish illusions that cloud the eyes of the unawakened!"

But Buck-Teeth shook his head slowly from side to side. "You don't understand, Kuro. Haiku died."

"What's that supposed to mean?"

"It died for me. I can't write it anymore."

"But it's your obligation to write, Buck-Teeth, to record the disaster that is life, to wake up others! It's your duty, your responsibility! Am I making sense? Do you follow me?"

"No," he said sadly, "I don't follow you." And he

walked away.

I hate seeing him like this—so long in the face, so listless.

That strange priest, Mud, talks loudly about visiting the "floating world" of pleasure, Yoshiwara. Kojiki shares his foolish excitement. It seems that they happened upon a pile of money in their travels and now yearn to waste it on the fleeting joys of the flesh. Today at tea, they urged Buck-Teeth to accompany them. He answered, morosely, "I've nothing better to do."

His stricken look made up my mind. I determined then and there to join their junket to Yoshiwara...to keep an eye on my friend.

It's the least I can do. Though he's an illusion inside Buddha's dream, destined to fade like the morning dew, I won't abandon him.

Some illusions matter more than others.

YOSHIWARA

KURO CAME WITH US to the pleasure district. This surprised me [that is, the me in Old Japan]. I didn't imagine the Poet in Black to be one who frequented fancy brothels, but perhaps I had misjudged him. Buck-Teeth came too, and Kojiki, strutting in the flashy new samurai armor that he had purchased in the capital that morning. He had wanted to buy a horse as well, but none of the ones he looked at had seemed "noble" enough, so he, like the rest of us, approached Yoshiwara on foot.

As we entered its tall gate spiked with sharpened bamboo, my heart started galloping in my chest.

"Where shall we go first?" I asked Kojiki, feeling as giddy as a kid at Disney World with a pass for all the rides.

But before he could answer, the gatekeeper shouted from his sentry shack, "You four, stop!"

"What's wrong?" Kojiki asked.

"A lady expects you."

"Lady? What lady?"

"Follow her." The gatekeeper pointed at a pretty waif of a girl who looked to be about eleven or twelve. She stood at the edge of the straw-covered road, watching us. She bowed—nervously, I thought—then walked away with small, shuffling steps.

We followed our little guide through throngs of pimps who were loudly touting the glories of their respective establishments. I felt almost as if I were back home on Bourbon Street, running a gauntlet of strip club hawkers. There, the doormen chant, "Cold Beer, hot women!"—but in Old Japan the advertising was much more poetic, like: "Come, friends, to the House of Sakura. Twenty fine, delicate jade blossoms, yours for the plucking!"

We soon reached a red mansion with a red sloping Chinese roof. The girl stopped and turned, making sure that we still followed. Then she, then we, stepped onto the verandah and kicked off our clogs or, in my case, Reeboks. The sun hadn't quite set, but two barefoot girls in blue kimonos stood on a railing, lighting red globe lanterns that dangled from the eaves.

Our guide turned to face us. "Please, sit. My mistress will join you soon."

As we settled onto straw mats, a geisha emerged from the house, knelt in a nearby corner, and began plucking her samisen, the elegant, long-necked banjo of Old Japan. Her plaintive, twanging song and expressionless face—like an ivory mask—mesmerized even Kuro.

I leaned over to Kojiki. "When do we pay?" In his acting days Kojiki had spent many a wild evening in Yoshiwara, he had bragged. He knew the protocol.

"This isn't that kind of place, priest," he whispered. "This house belongs to Edo's most extravagant courtesan, a consort of the Shogun himself."

"Why did she send for *us*?" I wondered.

"I don't know."

"Perhaps she's gotten wind of your money," Kuro suggested in a low voice.

"I don't see how," Kojiki said.

"A lady like that has spies. Watch yourselves," Kuro warned.

Then Buck-Teeth, who sat facing the door of the house, gasped. I read, in his easy-to-read face, sheer astonishment and helpless desire.

I turned and saw what he saw.

A woman stood in the doorway. She wore a flowing, blood-red kimono, her face powdered ghastly white. The mountain of black hair balanced on her head was riveted in place by a bewildering array of long, lacquered pins. The smile on her small, cherry mouth curved bewitchingly.

"Lady Plum," Kojiki said, "we are honored!"

* * *

LADY PLUM KNELT CLOSE to Buck-Teeth, very close. She bowed to each of us in turn, saying, "Welcome to my humble home."

With an almost imperceptible nod of her head, she summoned three gorgeous, giggling geisha from the house. One knelt near me, one near Kuro, and the third took her post at Kojiki's side. Lady Plum scooted even closer to Buck-Teeth.

"To what do we owe this pleasure?" Kojiki asked Lady Plum.

She ignored his question. "The Kabuki Theater has not been the same in the absence of the great Tora," she said, smiling sweetly.

Kojiki beamed. "So you know my stage name?"

Without answering, Lady Plum turned next to Buck-Teeth. "And what party would be complete without the inimitable poet who has given the world *Willow Moon* and *Invisible Cat*, my favorite collections? Buck-Teeth, your haiku are wonderful!"

"Thank you, Lady," he said with a sheepish smile. "I *was* a poet, once. But now—"

"No matter." She smoothly changed the subject.

"And you..." she looked at me dead-on with her brown, merry eyes, "You must be the priest they call Mud, no?"

I was flabbergasted that Lady Plum knew my so recently made-up name. Like Kojiki and Buck-Teeth had just done, I basked in the special attention that the glamorous courtesan bestowed.

Kuro, though, frowned.

Our hostess now addressed the Poet in Black. "But I wasn't expecting the great Kuro! What a treat it is that you have come down from your hermitage. I've admired your haiku for years."

"I'm glad they give you pleasure, Lady," Kuro, still frowning, said.

Kojiki asked, "How did you come to expect us, Lady Plum?"

The geisha who knelt at my side, an almond-eyed beauty in a shiny purple kimono, laughed.

Lady Plum laughed too. "Let's just say, I have my sources." She glanced at one of the servants who knelt nearby, the petite girl who had guided us to the mansion. The child hurried over, carrying a tray with a pitcher of sake and four small drinking cups. My geisha in purple took a cup, filled it to the brim, and raised it to my lips. The ones kneeling by Kojiki and Kuro did the same for them, and Lady Plum served a stunned, happy Buck-Teeth.

"Drink up, gentlemen," she said in a musical, lilting tone. "This night will be one to remember, I promise!"

THE BATH

MY GEISHA in the purple kimono was named Junko [pronounced "June" ko]. After pouring and feeding me several high-octane cups of sake, she asked, sweetly, "Won't you come into the house?"

Lady Plum smiled. "Yes, Junko. Show our guest, the priest, the hot tub. He'll find the water soothing, I'm sure."

Junko's large brown eyes, alluring and bright, beckoned me to my feet. She shimmied into the house, her hips working their sheath of purple silk like the pro she was. I followed. My imagination was racing fast-forward way past the hot bath to the hot sex that would surely follow. Scenes from erotic, Old Japanese pillow books danced in my head. As I visualized each fantastic, gymnastic sexual position, I replaced the blissful faces of the entwined lovers with mine and Junko's. My "jade peak" stirred.

Not all geisha have sex with customers, Kojiki had warned me earlier, but, he said, should one happen to invite me into the house, this would be a sure sign that lovemaking was in store. I glanced back at the party on the verandah. The samisen girl still plucked her sorrowful tune. Kuro's geisha lifted a sake cup to his frowning lips. Lady Plum and Buck-Teeth shared a silent conversation of eyes. Kojiki, red-faced and already soused, winked at me.

I entered the palace of pleasure.

* * *

THE WATER IN THE DEEP, wooden tub was almost scalding, but I eased my body down into it, first the toes, then the feet, then the legs...until, finally, even my chin whiskers soaked. Millions of pinpricks made millions of skin cells sigh, "Ahhh!" Only my head, above water, missed out on the tingling. Then Junko, from behind, doused it with a ladle.

"There," she cooed. "Does that please you?"

"Yes, Junko," I muttered. "It pleases me much."

Her fingers touched my neck, sending happy shivers down my spine. She began kneading my shoulders with the ruthless force of an expert masseuse.

"And this pleases you, too?" she asked huskily.

Oh yes, it pleased. But I couldn't say so. The sake in my belly, the steaming hot water up to my bottom lip, and Junko's relentless fingers had robbed me of speech. All I could manage was to nod and grunt.

The massage ended abruptly. "When you're through with your bath, please, lie on that quilt over there," she said. "I'll dry you."

She walked out of the room. I was pleasantly surprised to see that she had shed her kimono. Completely nude, her pale, curvaceous body might have been plagiarized from the pillow books that I had just been fantasizing about.

My jade peak demanded action. I clambered out of the tub and stretched belly down, dripping wet, on the thick, white quilt. I turned my head to one side and surrendered to gravity: the "corpse position" in yoga. Heart pounding, I awaited Junko's return.

Then, soft footsteps.

"I have a present for you. Stay still," she whispered in my ear.

I felt a tickle in that ear, then realized that she was pouring something into it, something cold and liquid. *She's a kinky one*, I thought. I opened my eyes and attempted to turn over...but couldn't. Couldn't move a muscle. Couldn't even close my eyes. I felt cold suddenly—cold as whatever she had filled my ear with...cold all over.

She laughed.

"The poison's working, I see. In a minute, priest, you'll be dead!"

Horror gripped the heart that beat slower and slower in the icebox of my chest. So cold, so cold, but I couldn't manage a shiver. And then, gradually, the coldness went away. I felt nothing then, absolutely nothing...not even my own existence.

Junko was right.

A minute later, I was dead.

PART THREE

HERO KURO

KURO WAS DRUNK but still Kuro. Though a fabulously beautiful woman was offering herself to him, urging him to come with her into the house for a "soothing bath," his serious mind forbade him to indulge. One by one the others had left the verandah—the priest, Kojiki, and Buck-Teeth—each in the company of a fetching courtesan. Of the three, Buck-Teeth seemed to have won first prize, for Lady Plum herself had escorted him into the mansion "to play poem cards," she had said, but Kuro knew what *that* meant.

Kuro's geisha whined, "Won't you go inside now? I want only to please you."

"Then pour me more sake," Kuro said. He hadn't felt this tipsy in years—not since the bad-old days when the Poet in Green, Mido, had made sure that his and Shiro's drinking cups stayed slopping-over full late into the moonlit evenings. To keep the party going, Mido would propose all sorts of absurd toasts and insist that his companions join him.

"To my fleas!" he would exclaim. *"Kampai!"*

Down the hatch.

"To *your* fleas!" Mido would toast. *"Kampai!"*

Down the hatch.

"And to their cousins! *Kampai!*"

Down the hatch.

"And second-cousins!"

And so on.

"Ah, Mido..." Kuro muttered fondly.

"My name is Haru!" The geisha pouted as she poured the sake.

"Just remembering an old friend." Kuro lifted his cup. "To Mido," he said softly.

Down the hatch.

"*Now* will you come?" Haru begged.

"You're wasting your breath, little one. You might as well run along. I'll be fine. I'll wait here for my companions."

Now Haru was at the point of tears. "My mistress will be angry if I fail to please you."

"Fine. Then tell your mistress, I'm *pleased* to sit here and wait for my friends."

"But... you can't!"

Kuro's trademark frown, which had nearly vanished while reminiscing about Mido and bygone days, returned full force. "What do you mean, I can't? What's going on? Tell me!" He grabbed Haru's arm.

Tears fell. "Nothing. I... I don't know what you're talking about!"

"Why are you so eager to get me inside?"

"You're hurting me!"

"What's going on in there?"

Suddenly, Kuro thought of Buck-Teeth. Was he in danger?

"Take me to Buck-Teeth!" he hissed.

"I can't. I—"

"Take me now!" Kuro stood, yanking the geisha to her feet.

* * *

IN THE FIRST ROOM he checked, Kuro found my body. I lay on the white quilt, naked, beer-belly down, my head twisted to one side. My glassy green eyes wide open, I looked astonished. Kuro crouched to touch my neck, confirming the obvious. Cold. Dead.

The poor devil wasn't expecting this, he mused [quite correctly] then stood and shook Haru, hard.

"Who did this?"

"I can't say."

"The others. Where are they? Where's Buck-Teeth?"

Between sobs, Haru whimpered, "Up there." She

pointed at a staircase.

Kuro let her go and raced up the steps, his night-black *yukata* flying. He stormed down the corridor, found a paper door to the left, threw it open.

In a room lit by a single, sputtering lamp he found Kojiki. The beggar-bodyguard lay on his back, naked as I had been. But Kojiki's flesh flushed pink with life. A geisha straddled him, riding wildly, her cupcake breasts bouncing.

Kojiki moaned with delight. The courtesan's long black hair, free of its chopstick pins, flapped like the wings of a mad raven.

She leaned forward, dropping a nipple into Kojiki's eager mouth. Her hand, meanwhile, slipped under the futon and...

"Watch out!" Kuro yelled.

Kojiki jerked the pillow from under his head and thrust it over his face, snagging the knife just as it came slashing down. He shoved the geisha aside and rolled to his feet. Yanking the weapon from the pillow, he leveled it at her throat. "Little girls shouldn't play with sharp things," he growled.

"We've got to warn Buck-Teeth!" Kuro urged. "The priest is dead!"

"Your mistress's room..." Kojiki pressed the dagger's tip against the girl's neck, drawing a dot of blood. "Where is it?"

FLEMING

WITH ALL THE EXCITEMENT going on in Old Japan, I haven't found the time to mourn my recent death. That geisha Junko stole a page out of *Hamlet*, dropping a "mixture rank" into my ear. I've got to hand it to her, though; she had me completely fooled. But then, I've never been a good judge of women. Exhibit A: my ex-fiancée in Massachusetts who swatted my heart like a fly and now didn't care I existed.

In the kind of coincidence that only happens in real life, too bizarre for fiction, one morning, recently, that same ex-fiancée, Natasha, phoned at five a.m.

"Guess what?" she asked.

"What?"

"I have a baby."

"Congratulations."

"A baby boy."

"That's nice."

"Yeah. Can you believe it?"

"I believe it."

"Just thought you'd like to know."

I said nothing to this, my groggy mind still half-convinced that this was all part of the dream I had been having just before the phone rang, something about walruses loose in a fancy hotel.

"We named him Fleming."

"That's nice," I muttered.

"Everyone says he looks like Bruno."

"So you're still together?"

"We're working at it."

"Work hard. Fleming'll need his mommy *and* his daddy."

She said nothing for a moment, then remarked, casually, "I'll be in New Orleans this weekend."

"Yeah?"

"Visiting my parents. Want to see him?"

"Him?"

"The baby."

"Why not?" I said, biting my lip. I didn't want her to know that my heart felt like it was being squeezed in a vise. Be cool, I told myself, but I quickly lost my cool and blurted, "Is that why we broke up? You wanted kids? I could've had the vasectomy reversed!"

"That wasn't it," she said softly.

"Then why? I need to know. Why, Natasha? Why

did you dump me?"

Silence on the line.

"Natasha?"

"Let's talk in person. Saturday. I'll call in the afternoon. What time's good for you?" she asked.

"Two o'clock?"

"Great. Two o'clock. I'll call. We'll meet somewhere."

"Cool. And Natasha, I'm happy for you. I mean that."

"See you Saturday."

* * *

SATURDAY ROLLED AROUND. Two o'clock became three...became four. Natasha, true to form, didn't call.

I didn't meet little Fleming.

THE WRITING GROUP CATCHES UP

"COOL!" Chaz commented first. "At last, some action."

It had taken months, but my writing group had finally caught up with my writing. Now, their guesses were as good as mine as to what the Buddha would inspire me to scribble next on the clean, blank page...*this* page.

Chaz's favorable reaction didn't surprise me, since his own fiction tends to the violent and gore-spattered side of the spectrum. I smiled, pleased that at least one group member approved of this week's chapters. But Micky and Paul, with poker faces, said nothing. In their silence, Chaz added, "But don't wander off the subject. No more digressions about ex-girlfriends! Stick to the action. Will they reach Buck-Teeth in time? Will he die, too? And I want a *decent* fight scene. Kojiki should kick that ninja's ass."

"You think so?" I asked.

He nodded emphatically, his silver sword earring bouncing. "You've raised certain expectations in the reader's mind, a check that now you'd better cash. Just stick to the formula."

"Formula?"

He clucked his tongue. "As if you didn't know you're writing a western! Your broken-down samurai, he's the old gunslinger sobering up for one last showdown. But he'll win; he has to. He'll whoop that Nakamura."

Micky sighed. "Well, this reader, for one, will be disappointed if the novel degenerates to a Hollywood formula." She intoned the word, "*Hollywood*," most derisively. "And I certainly don't want to see Professor Nakamura 'whooped,' as you so delicately put it," she told Chaz.

Micky's attitude mystified me. From the moment that Professor Nakamura had crept into this book, she had responded peevishly to everything I had written about him. When she read the part about the dagger he hurled at my face in the cedar forest, she had muttered, "Really!" And later, when I shared the scene describing his clandestine meeting with Lady Plum on the Shogun's shadowy verandah, Micky had rolled her bright eyes.

"What's wrong?" I had asked.

"I didn't realize you were writing melodrama," she said with a smirk.

Why was she being so...testy?

"Tell me about him," I now said.

"I beg your pardon?"

"Professor Nakamura. Tell me about him."

She looked puzzled.

"You said you met at a conference? That you co-chaired a panel?"

"Yes, but—"

"Then you know him. Tell me about him, Micky. Fill me in on his habits, his quirks. You've accused me of caricaturing him, so help me get it right. Help me make him real. What's his favorite color? What does he do for fun?"

"What's in his refrigerator?" Chaz joined in.

"Boxers or briefs?" Paul asked, looking at Micky with a steady, strangely serious gaze.

"What?!" she gasped, and then I realized what Paul must have already, somehow, guessed: she knew the answer!

My jaw dropped. "You mean you *slept* with him?"

"I don't see how that's any of your business," she snapped.

In the long, tense pause that followed, I contemplated the situation. A writing group colleague having sex with one of my characters seemed downright...incestuous! I stared at the bright, abstract cover of one of the obscure foreign paperbacks that always cluttered Micky's coffee table, too embarrassed to meet her eyes.

It was up to her to break the awful silence. Finally, she did so, with a sigh.

"Boxers," she said.

THE TEARS OF A LADY

THEY FOUND BUCK-TEETH NAKED, gagged and hog-tied on the floor of one of the upper rooms. While Kojiki, also still naked, cut the ropes with the knife that he had snatched from his would-be assassin, Kuro interrogated Lady Plum.

"Who put you up to this?"

"I don't know," she said, her eyes glistening tears. "He's a ninja."

"A ninja? And is he coming? Tonight? Is that why you've gift-wrapped Buck-Teeth?"

Lady Plum nodded, sobbing.

"Save your tears, woman," Kuro snarled.

"I say let's kill her. Kill them all." Kojiki helped Buck-Teeth to his feet.

"No!" Buck-Teeth exclaimed. "What good would that do? Let's just go!"

"You don't understand, Buck-Teeth. They murdered the priest. The one I vowed to protect." Kojiki glowered at Lady Plum, raising the knife. He pointed its blood-daubed tip at the courtesan.

She laughed through her tears. "I'm sorry, but if you're going to kill me, could you please put something on?"

"Yes, get dressed, both of you," Kuro advised. "If that ninja's on his way, we'd best get going."

Kojiki sighed and lowered the blade. "Keep an eye on her." He left the room.

Buck-Teeth found his *yukata* bundled in a corner. He threw on the garment and tied its sash 'round his waist in a hasty knot. He bent to collect his travel satchel. But it felt different, lighter.

"My money's gone!"

"Good riddance," Kuro said. "Such wealth only brings trouble. Look what it did for the priest."

Lady Plum approached Kuro and touched his black sleeve. "Take me with you."

"What?"

"Take me when you go."

"You must be joking!"

Big, pendulous tears rolled slowly down her cheeks, plowing twin furrows through the white powder of her make-up. "He'll kill me. He swore to, if I failed. You *must* take me!"

Kuro pushed her away. "You know the punishment if we help you leave the district."

"I know."

"And we should risk *our* lives for you? Life's

short enough. Accept your karma."

Kojiki, fully clothed now and adjusting the lacquered bamboo breastplate of his samurai armor, appeared in the doorway. "Let's get out of here!"

Lady Plum buried her face in fluttering hands and wept.

Kuro started for the door.

"We can't leave her," Buck-Teeth said.

Kuro turned and looked at his young friend in disbelief.

"*I* can't leave her," Buck-Teeth added.

"But you must!"

Buck-Teeth didn't budge.

Kojiki stepped into the room. "After what she did to you, Buck-Teeth, you would help her?"

"I won't leave her to the ninja."

Kojiki sighed. He strolled over to Lady Plum, casually drawing his long sword, the *katana*, with a hiss. With his free hand he grabbed hold of her piled-high hair. He pulled on it hard, jerking back her head.

"No!" Buck-Teeth yelled.

The *katana's* blade fell—*swoosh*—chopstick pins flying in all directions, clattering to the floor. A fluffy black cloud, Lady Plum's hair, floated softly, softly down.

"Well, it's a start," Kojiki said. He handed her a knife.

She stood frozen, staring down at her midnight tresses that lay scattered at her bare feet. She turned the knife around—slowly, solemnly—so that its point touched her throat, dead center. She took a deep breath and squeezed the hilt so tightly her knuckles turned white. She tensed her arms.

"Not that!" Kojiki smiled, resting his hands over Lady Plum's. Though she had proven herself an enemy, he admired her samurai spirit. "Cut off the rest of your hair, and be quick about it!"

She gave him a bewildered look.

"And when you're done, put on the robe of the priest you had killed. If you're coming with us, you'll come in disguise."

WORDLESS

THE YEAR'S FIRST SNOWFALL blanketed the ground and draped the willows. The Poet in White, nearly invisible in all that whiteness, savored a wonderful silence.

He was mentally conjuring a haiku about snow and silence when he heard muffled footsteps...

* * *

BEFORE I NARRATE the arrival of Kuro, Kojiki, Buck-Teeth, and the now-bald Lady Plum, I have the urge to translate the poem that Shiro was just now imagining, but this might prove difficult. After all, Shiro's poetry was always wordless. How can I capture it in words?

I probably can't, but I'll try. Close your eyes and picture thick, luscious snow, two-feet deep, covering hills and fields and sagging willow trees.

Now picture yourself in the scene, part of the scene, alone, walking. The crispy surface of the snow gives way to fluffy softness as your boots crunch and sink, crunch and sink. Now, stop.

Be still. Listen to the hush, a hush so hushed, it roars!

Hold all these sensations in your heart-mind but don't allow words, even imagined ones, to spoil the moment by attempting to describe it or explain it or define it. Do this for a good ten seconds—fifteen if you can manage—and you'll have at least an inkling of the actual content of Shiro's silent haiku that day.

* * *

HE GREETED HIS GUESTS with a smile that said, "I'm happy to see you. Please, do come inside. Sorry the place is a mess!" His nonverbal messages were always this clear. Ever since he abandoned human speech years ago, the Poet in White had learned to use face and hands to express, more quickly and less problematically than ordinary talking, whatever he felt or thought in any given moment.

"We're so glad to find you at home, old friend," Kuro said. "Please, allow me to introduce my companions. Buck-Teeth, of course, you know. And

Kojiki, our former bodyguard, now wears samurai armor. He came into some money lately, but that's another story. And this...nun, she's a traveler seeking Buddha's salvation. Her name is Plum."

Shiro bowed to "Nun Plum," upon whose petite body my large, saffron robe hung limply. She had knotted it to cover both shoulders, nun-like. Her face, washed clean of geisha makeup, was still stunning with sparkling brown eyes and soft, pouting lips.

She returned Shiro's bow.

Turning to Kuro, Shiro widened his eyes to form a question.

Kuro understood. "The priest? Oh, he's fine. We parted ways recently."

Not owning a suspicious bone in his body, Shiro accepted Kuro's lie that I was alive and well. Kuro had warned the others, before they arrived at Shiro's hut, that it would be best if they didn't mention what had transpired back in Yoshiwara. He especially didn't want Shiro to know that the "nun" with them was a fugitive courtesan. In her former life, Lady Plum had traveled freely outside of the spiked enclosure of Yoshiwara, but always encased in her palanquin, whose bearers were sworn to return her to the pleasure district. Leaving the district without such escort was a grave crime. By now, the Shogun's samurai would be searching high and low for Lady Plum. The Poet in White, childlike in his innocence, was incapable of subterfuge. If interrogated, his eyes simply could not keep secrets. "We'll not tell him," Kuro had advised the others, "for his own good."

In the center of the hut, a wood fire crackled in the sunken hearth. The four new arrivals huddled around it, warming their hands while Shiro filled an iron kettle with water. He slipped its handle onto the pothook that dangled over the flame, then looked up inquisitively.

"Yes, I'll have tea," Kuro answered.

"I shall, too," Buck-Teeth said.

"Yes, thank you," Kojiki said.

Nun Plum nodded.

Soon they were sipping hot green tea, the only sounds in the room their slurps and swallows. Keeping their promise not to talk about recent events, the visitors didn't quite know what to say. Shiro, however, felt none of the awkwardness that the others did. In fact, he savored this blissful absence of language. To him, it was the best tea ceremony ever.

Afterwards, Kuro and Kojiki took a walk in the snow.

"It's foolish, protecting that woman," Kuro said.

"True. But we had to take her. How else would we have gotten Buck-Teeth to leave?"

They stopped where the whiteness met a river's cold, black flow.

Kuro shook his head from side to side. "The boy worries me. Just when I thought he was maturing philosophically, he quits haiku and attaches himself to a murderess."

"He's not the only one to fall under *her* spell. As I recall, she had all of us fooled."

Kuro frowned. "You may think so if you wish. But I only played along. I never trusted her."

"Then you're wiser than I. She caught me completely off guard."

"You're in good company," Kuro said. "Even the great Lord Kaga was reduced to a naked hermit, thanks to Lady Plum. And now he begs on the slope of Mount Fuji."

Kojiki gasped. "I thought that was just a myth!"

"No. It's true. Buck-Teeth and I visited him there once, years ago."

"Is that so? And is he still up there?"

"I suppose."

They strolled along the riverbank, crunching the ice-glazed snow. Suddenly, Kojiki stopped. "Of course!" he said.

"What?"

Kojiki drew his *katana* and took a few whooshing practice swipes in the air. "How would you feel about visiting Mount Fuji?"

"In this weather?"

Kojiki hacked off the snow-burdened branch of a willow. It fell noiselessly to the ground, a billion white flakes swirling and glittering in the afternoon light.

"Fuji's a fine place to hide. No one climbs it this time of year. And if Lord Kaga's still up there, he might appreciate seeing his lady-love again. He might even take her off our hands."

Kuro frowned. "Climb Mount Fuji in avalanche season?"

Kojiki sheathed his sword. "Lady Plum's a far greater danger. The sooner we get rid of her, the better."

A MAD PROPOSAL

"IT CAN'T BE DONE in wintertime!" Kuro insisted. But his dire warnings, all afternoon, fell on deaf ears. Kojiki's mad proposal that they climb Mount Fuji, despite the season, "and visit the holy man who lives there," excited the others. Shiro, a lover of snow, could hardly wait to get started. His enthusiasm was infectious, and even brought a smile to Buck-Teeth's easily-read face. Lady Plum also favored the idea, though she, unlike the men, had never climbed a mountain before, let alone in wintertime, and was clueless as to how strenuous it would be. Still, Kojiki appreciated her vote. He mused with a malicious grin, *She deserves the aches and frost-bite of a hard climb. May her toes fall off!*

"We'll go tomorrow at first light," he said out loud.

* * *

Buck-Teeth and Kojiki went into Edo to buy snow gear—heavy coats, boots and such—leaving Shiro, Kuro, and the bald "Nun Plum" huddled around the fire. After a while, without explanation, Shiro stood and left the hut.

Kuro sat across the sunken hearth directly across from the woman wrapped in the baggy saffron robe. A long silence ensued, broken only by the sputtering flames. Kuro cleared his throat.

"Yes?" she asked, arching her perfect eyebrows.

"Nothing."

"Oh, I thought you were about to say something."

"No." Kuro grimaced. He felt tense, being left alone with the courtesan. What new treachery was she plotting, even now, as she sat smiling at him through the rising smoke?

Shiro, just then, burst into the hut, his eyes wildly excited.

"What is it? The ninja?" Kuro jumped to his feet.

The Poet in White smiled, indicating that his excitement was of the happy, not fearful, sort. He made it known through vigorous hand gestures that he wanted Kuro and Lady Plum to follow him outside.

Which they did. In the clearing in front of the hut, Shiro pointed at something new: a pot-bellied Buddha made of snow.

"Not bad," Kuro said.

Lady Plum giggled. "May I make one too?" she asked in a little girl's voice as if begging a grown-up for permission to play. Shiro nodded enthusiastically.

She began scooping and patting soft, mushy snow into her Buddha's first stage, the legs and lap. While she happily worked, Kuro commented, "How apt. In this fading, dewdrop universe, even Lord Buddha is here today, a puddle of water tomorrow. Nothing abides."

Shiro sighed.

Kuro continued. "I'm reminded of our master's haiku,

even our fleeting snow
becomes
Buddha!

Remember it?"

Shiro nodded and smiled.

"I recall the day he wrote it. Master Cup-of-Tea insisted that each of us build a snow Buddha. But only when our work was done did its meaning sink in. Without breathing a word, he had taught us all an eloquent lesson in *mujô*: everything in this shitty world, even the Buddha, eventually melts to nothingness."

The Poet in White didn't at all agree with the

Poet in Black's serious interpretation of snow Buddhas. For Shiro, making them had nothing to do with lessons about life's transience. He just thought it was fun.

As did, evidently, Lady Plum, who punctuated her snow-patting with childlike laughter. Kuro, watching her, shook his head sadly. "She just doesn't get it," he muttered.

Shiro shook his head too, thinking the same thing about Kuro.

LADY PLUM TALKS TO BUCK-TEETH WHILE THEY CLIMB MOUNT FUJI

All day you've kept quiet, as quiet as the one you call Shiro. Only, his silence isn't troubling. His mouth makes no sound, yet he talks quite a lot—with his eyes, his smiles, his gentle hands. But you, Buck-Teeth, your eyes say nothing. Why?

I've heard that you've given up writing. They say that haiku is dead for you, now, like that cat you wrote about:

in the dead cat's eyes
harvest
moons

Finally, a reaction! The night we met, I wasn't lying when I said that I love your haiku. I've memorized many of your poems, Buck-Teeth. What else was there to do, those long, dreary years in my prison?

Oh yes, Yoshiwara *was* a prison. But I'd rather not talk about it.

You have a gift, Buck-Teeth. People need you to use your gift, your talent. I have a talent, too, or at least had one, but my forte, entertaining gentlemen, bestowing pleasure—ecstasy even—leaves not a trace in the world. When my work is done, the customer swaggers away into the night, and I feel empty. I wonder, sometimes, what it would be like to be the wife he swaggers home to.

I wish I could do what you do, Buck-Teeth, send ripples of joy, like dropping a stone in a pond, touching others, faraway people...making them happy.

A silly dream for a whore.

Yes, I said "whore." I realize it's an unladylike word, but I'm not a lady, not anymore. Walking in this snow, my hair gone, all my pretty kimonos just memories, I don't know exactly *what* I am. I certainly don't feel like the 'nun' I'm supposed to be. Or am I a monk, should anyone ask? Kuro said women aren't allowed here on Mount Fuji; it's a place too holy for *us*!

All my life I've gazed at this mountain but always from far away. When I was a little girl growing up in Yoshiwara, I daydreamed about it all the time. I imagined it was a paradise filled with happy snow fairies. So now, to be climbing it—

What's wrong? You look troubled. Did anyone ever tell you, Buck-Teeth, your face is easy to read? You're sad, aren't you? Sad that I grew up in Yoshiwara. It's true. My mother was a courtesan. My father, she claimed, had imperial blood, but she never mentioned his name. Perhaps she was lying. Perhaps she didn't know *which* customer he was.

Yes, Buck-Teeth, I've spent my whole life in that prison you poets call the "floating world of pleasure." Trained from childhood to do what I do, to entertain men...and control them.

And I'm good at it. My being here proves that. After all I did to you—tricking you, tying you up for the ninja—you still wanted to protect me, risking your life to get me to a safe place. Mother taught me well!

Don't misunderstand me, though. That ninja was going to kill me. When he came near on the Shogun's verandah, the night I met him, I knew he was bad news. He felt...like an icy presence, like a hungry ghost, like...death.

But I'm not at all like him. Yes, I would have let him have you, but this is only because I had no other option—I was so afraid. And he promised to pay me well. He told me all about the money that you, the samurai and the priest had found. He said I could keep it, if I succeeded. But if I failed...

I apologize for deceiving you. If truth be told, I

was just about to give you a bit of...joy when your friends showed up. I felt it was the least I could do.

Don't blush. I've seen it all, heard it all. But I've *done* practically nothing. That's why I'm so happy to be here, climbing this mountain, free!

You need to be happy, too. And I know just what should do the trick.

Write me a haiku, Buck-Teeth! I've always wanted someone to make a poem, a perfect little jewel of words, just for me. Many have tried. All have failed. But you, Buck-Teeth, *you* could do it. Write me a haiku. Make me happy. Make yourself happy.

A poet is happiest, making poems.

Am I right?

SUSHI WITH A FORK

BUCK-TEETH WANTED BADLY to please Lady Plum, but he had never been able to compose poetry on demand, even back in the days before haiku died for him. Then, inspiration had come spontaneously or not at all. These days, it came not at all, period.

"I'm sorry, lady," he mumbled.

"Well, take your time. I'm sure you'll think of something. And remember, I'm not a lady anymore," she chirped.

Had haiku still lived for Buck-Teeth, there would have been plenty of subject matter for it, as he, Kojiki, Shiro, Kuro, and the former lady, Plum, on the last day of the year, climbed Mount Fuji's eastern slope. The deep, sparkling snow, the ice-slicked, zigzagging path, and a half-buried stone Buddha that they stumbled upon—all would have had the old Buck-Teeth reaching excitedly for brush and ink-stone. The new Buck-Teeth only sighed. The forlorn, icy Buddha reminded him of his master's haiku,

from the tip
of the field Buddha's nose...
an icicle

. . . but even Cup-of-Tea's poetry now seemed lifeless to his former star student. The ninja had fatally opened his eyes. A haiku was nothing but a hollow sequence of sounds: *chimpunkan*, empty babble.

Buck-Teeth felt sorry for the woman. She wanted so badly to have a poem written in her honor. He remembered his first summer of haiku instruction in the meadow behind Cup-of-Tea's Trash House. Lord Kaga had joined them one shocking afternoon, and every day for a hundred days thereafter the fearsome daimyo had labored to write a gift poem for his then-mistress, the then-Lady Plum. But, as she told Buck-Teeth, "Many have tried. All have failed." Lord Kaga had been one of those failures, and now he shivered somewhere on this frozen mountain. Or had he died?

As if reading Buck-Teeth's thought, Kojiki, who led the expedition, turned and remarked, "I don't see how he survives in this weather, that Kaga."

"All things pass," Kuro commented gravely.

But the hopeful expression on Shiro's wind-reddened face showed that *he* was convinced that Kaga still lived.

Kuro shook his head. "Always the optimist."

* * *

FINAL EXAMS BEGAN and winter break was just around the corner. Procrastinating as usual, I nevertheless managed to book super-saver airfare to my *furusato* ["native village"] of Omaha, Nebraska. Soon, I would be devouring Mom's peanut brittle, shooting pool with Dad in the basement, and playing "tickle spider" with my squealing nieces and nephews.

But first there was much busywork to deal with: forbidding stacks of final portfolios to grade. I had to put this book on hold. Next week, I promised myself, we'd see what happens up there on Mount Fuji.

I prayed that my muse, the Buddha, would understand. My teaching job had to come first, at least for the time being. After all, it kept a roof over my head and put food on the table—the latter being just an expression, since I didn't eat at the kitchen table, it being hopelessly buried under mounds of scribbled pages. I took my meals on the futon in the bedroom, legs crossed, eyes locked on my little TV. Though I could easily reach its buttons, I preferred the remote, restlessly zapping from channel to channel as I chewed.

Such was life in my upstairs shotgun apartment in Mid-City, New Orleans, as the days grew short and the nights chilly and long.

One such long, chilly night, I stayed up till dawn, grading the last pile of portfolios and calculating final grades. Feeling euphoric to be approaching the end, I was perhaps a bit too generous, but my students weren't likely to complain. At eight a.m., tired but triumphant, I pedaled my bike to the little college campus in Mid-City, turned in my grades and, before heading home, stopped at my office to collect a few things.

The phone's light was blinking. There was a message.

I punched in my code and retrieved: "This is Dr. Nakamura at Uptown University. I'd like very much to meet with you. There's a vital matter I'd like to discuss, if you're available."

I was stunned. Professor Nakamura, who had so rudely evicted me from his office, now wanted to see me? *Why?*

At the end of his message he left a number. I gritted my teeth and dialed.

* * *

We met at my favorite uptown sushi restaurant. After we settled in our seats, wiping our hands with the steaming towels provided, Professor Nakamura spoke.

"I suppose you're wondering why I wanted to meet with you." His voice was like crispy snow. "It concerns your book."

"My book?"

Before he could explain, a kimono-clad waitress shuffled up, inquiring about our drink orders.

"Water," he said.

"I'd like a beer. Do you have Kirin?"

"Yes."

"Make it a large."

"And miss," Professor Nakamura waved at the waitress as she turned to go, "bring me a fork."

Perhaps he read astonishment in my face. Addressing me, he said, "I find the fork to be a most convenient utensil."

I tore my chopsticks out of their paper wrapper and set them on the table.

He ignored my defiant gesture. "So, back to my point," he continued. "As I'm sure you know, I've been commissioned to review your manuscript."

"You *have*?" Earlier that year, brimming with optimism, I had mailed several copies of my first book—the prequel to this one—to publishers. Most of those copies had already found their way home to my mailbox, along with heart-squeezing rejection notes. To-date, two or three remained at large.

"Who commissioned you?" I asked.

"I'm not at liberty to say. In fact, my review is to be strictly confidential. Ordinarily, I would simply mail it off and be done with it, but in light of my acquaintance with...a colleague of yours—"

"Oh, you mean Micky?"

His eyes widened with surprise. He cleared his throat. "Ahem, yes. I am referring to Professor Greenfeld. And in deference to her, I thought that, perhaps, a face-to-face meeting might help clear up certain aspects of your work that I find... troubling."

"Troubling?"

The waitress brought Nakamura's water and my beer. I glugged down a good amount of the latter and then, fortified, said, "Before we get to that, I have a question."

"Yes?"

"When I visited your office last September, why did you go off on me?"

"Go off?"

"Go off, freak out. You know what I mean."

"I'm afraid that I don't."

I shrugged. "You seemed upset. You asked me to leave. Why?"

He smiled wanly. "Surely you understand that! I naturally assumed, when you mentioned your book, that you had come to lobby for it. I had just received it that week. I didn't want to be unduly influenced by anything that you might have said, at least, not until I read it."

"Oh." I felt guilty, suddenly, for having made Professor Nakamura into an evil ninja. His explanation sounded so...sensible!

"I didn't know you were my reviewer," I muttered.

"You didn't?"

"I only wanted to ask a question...about that four-and-a-half month gap in Buck-Teeth's diary."

"My goodness," he said, "I misjudged you!"

Our waitress reappeared, we ordered our lunches, and Professor Nakamura launched into his interrogation.

"My first difficulty with your text is categorizing it. Is it a novel, a how-to book, or literary criticism?"

"Does it *need* to be categorized?" I asked, hoping to avoid a question for which I had no answer.

He gave me a look that said, *Of course it does*!

He added, out loud, "If you cooperate I might be disposed to submit a positive recommendation. If, for example, you claim your text is literary criticism, I will suggest that you eliminate all that extraneous business about your personal life. On the other hand, if it's a novel you're attempting, I shall recommend, in the strongest of terms, that you delete all nonfiction elements. Frankly, I find it distracting, the way you mingle fancy with fact."

"What do you mean?"

"I could cite dozens of examples," he said, just as our food arrived: two large boats of assorted sushi and sashimi. "For instance, you state that Cup-of-Tea returned to live in his native village—an historical fact. But then you say that this happened forty years after his leaving home."

"So?"

Nakamura clucked his tongue. "Cup-of-Tea was in exile for *thirty-seven* years!" He leaned back in his chair and crossed his arms, an expression of smug triumph on his face.

"I just rounded off the number," I mumbled, dipping a California roll in soy sauce. *What an asshole*, I thought.

Professor Nakamura speared a gleaming, red hunk of tuna with his fork. "And let's not overlook the fact that you have your characters going about in bathrobes everywhere...or your odd claim that Buck-Teeth enjoyed a 'long, poetically productive life'."

"But he did!"

Nakamura smirked. "If you have read any of my books, you will know that haiku as a form lost its vigor long before Buck-Teeth reached his latter years."

"I'm familiar with your theory," I said, chewing a cold, salty-squishy roll of salmon roe sushi. "But, with due respect, I disagree. Haiku didn't die in Old Japan. It's alive and well, and being written all over the place, even right here in the Crescent City. Why, in this very restaurant, at that table over there, some buddies and I had a *renga* party not too long ago, writing haiku and drinking into the wee hours. Isn't that proof enough?"

Evidently, it wasn't. The words, "Not recommended for publication," flashed like dark neon in his hard, unblinking eyes. Whatever favor he felt he owed Micky would not be paid through me.

No matter, I thought. *I'll deal with you, professor, in the climax!*

I chugged my beer and glared at the world-famous scholar.

THE GROTTO

"ARE WE CLOSE?" The former lady, Plum, shivered and suffered. Her faraway mountain of snow fairies was turning out to be a steep, wretched, frozen wasteland. The howling wind stung her face and fingers. Her feet were numb stones.

"Keep walking," Kojiki said sternly. "Walk or you'll freeze!"

"It's not far, I think," Kuro said. "though the first time Buck-Teeth and I came this way, it was spring. We didn't have all this damn snow to contend with. Everything looks...different now."

Shiro smiled, reveling in the "damn snow." The blizzard had completely erased the horizon. Heaven and earth melded into one pure, blinding-white blankness—most pleasing to Shiro.

Buck-Teeth shouted, "Look!"

All eyes squinted in the direction he pointed, but nothing appeared but a solid curtain of snow. Then, for a fleeting instant, the wind died a little and a grotto of dark, glistening boulders materialized in the near distance.

"That's it!" Buck-Teeth hollered over the wind that snapped the white curtain shut again.

"I hope he has a fire," Kojiki said.

"I hope he's *alive*," Kuro said.

Shiro plunged off the trail into the chest-deep snow, wading in the direction that Buck-Teeth had pointed.

"Follow him, everyone!" Kojiki shouted.

They followed, single file, in the furrow plowed by the Poet in White's body. Soon, chest-deep snow became waist-deep snow, and then, knee-deep. By the time the group reached the grotto of craggy black rocks and blasted pines, the snow had given way to ankle-deep slush. Rain trickled from a white, luminous sky. And, incredibly, the rain felt warm.

Buck-Teeth peeled off his heavy coat.

"Don't!" Kojiki hollered.

"But I'm hot!"

Lady Plum also removed her winter coat, then kicked off her boots. In her wet, baggy robe she whirled and danced gleefully, her bare feet splashing puddles.

"It feels wonderful!" She giggled.

"It's witchery!" Kojiki warned. "This can't be real."

For miles in all directions, Mount Fuji was enveloped in snow. But in this one place the swirling flakes above were melting and dropping as big, warm raindrops.

Buck-Teeth ventured farther into the rain-slicked maze of boulders and fallen trees. Soon, a soft voice stopped him in his tracks.

"You're back!"

"Lord Kaga?" Buck-Teeth gasped. The voice was Lord Kaga's, but the apparition to whom it seemed to belong looked nothing like the man that Buck-Teeth remembered. Naked he sat, cross-legged on a ledge of rock, a mane of wet, black hair wriggling down his back. His once-powerful chest was lumpy with ribs. The bones in his legs looked like brittle, knobby bamboo. But the most amazing thing about him was his *glow*. From head to toe, his whole body radiated bright orange light, as if thousands of tiny, roiling fires raged just beneath the surface of his translucent skin.

"I told you the last time you came, Buck-Teeth, I'm not a lord anymore." Kaga grinned, his facial skin clinging to his skull like shrink-wrap.

Buck-Teeth shouted to the others, "I found him!" Then he approached the glowing holy man. As he did so, the pelting rain felt warmer and warmer. When he reached the clearing where Kaga sat, rain gave way to a hissing cloud of steam.

The second person to enter Kaga's sauna, dancing and giggling, was "Nun Plum."

Buck-Teeth, a stickler for politeness, said, "I'd like to introduce—"

"A hermit," Kaga interrupted. "That's my only name, now."

"Pleased to meet you, Hermit," the woman said cheerfully. "Nice place you have here. It's so warm!"

Hermit Kaga nodded and glowed a bit brighter.

"And Hermit," Buck-Teeth said, "please, allow me to introduce—"

"A nun." Now *she* interrupted. "I agree with Mr. Hermit. What use have we for names?"

"Come, sit near me, Nun." The glowing hermit who was once Lord Kaga, terrible lord of Shinano Province, patted the wet stone ledge next to him.

"Don't mind if I do." The nun, once the ravishing Lady Plum, high courtesan and consort of the Shogun, took her seat in the hot womb of steam.

Black-robed Kuro arrived next and stood by Buck-Teeth. He whispered, "Do they recognize each other?"

"I don't think so."

"Amazing!"

Buck-Teeth smiled. "But they seem to be getting on well."

Then Kojiki and Shiro stepped into the cloud.

"It's witchery, I tell you!" Kojiki exclaimed.

Shiro, catching sight of the fiery hermit, gasped...then giggled.

Kojiki clutched the hilt of his sword.

"This is who we came to see!" Buck-Teeth hastened to say. "He's our friend, the hermit."

Kojiki released his grip on his weapon—slowly—and bowed, regaining his composure. "We've climbed all this way, Sir Hermit, and through a terrible storm, to ask a great favor of you. This woman, this nun, needs a place to hide, a refuge from the dangerous world. We thought that perhaps..."

Kaga raised a hand, showing its fiery palm. All five fingernails, eight to nine inches long, curled like wild corkscrews. "Say no more. I, too, have become a seeker of Buddha's peace. My little sister is welcome to stay as long as she likes."

The former heartbreaker and former heartbroken sat side by side. She was bald and smiling. He was naked and bony, a bright, living furnace. Though they shared a past, neither one remembered it, now. And anyway, the past didn't matter. It never had mattered, really.

They make a nice couple, Buck-Teeth thought, smiling from ear to ear.

AND THEN...

"*THAT* WAS ODD," Kojiki said.

"Very odd," Kuro agreed.

Shiro shrugged his shoulders, said nothing.

Buck-Teeth, smiling hugely, said, "I didn't find it *too* odd!"

The four of them, back in their heavy winter coats, stomped and slid down the frozen trail. Kuro was preparing to say something appropriately sobering to his young, naïve friend when a dark figure stepped into their path.

"Shadow warrior!" Kojiki drew his *katana*.

"That won't be necessary," the ninja said, opening both hands to show that he held no weapons. "I've come to say goodbye. My work here is done."

"Your work?" Kojiki, crouched in battle pose, eyed the ninja suspiciously.

Professor Nakamura fixed his cold, dark gaze on Buck-Teeth. "I know what you saw up there, Buck-Teeth. The frozen grotto. The wolf-gnawed bones of your old, good friend, Lord Kaga. *Reality*, Buck-Teeth! It's painful, but necessary."

Buck-Teeth chuckled. "Is *that* what you think I saw?"

The ninja seemed confused. "It's hardly a laughing matter..."

And then Shiro started laughing, too. Kojiki joined in.

"But, but he *is* dead up there. He *has* to be! It's an incontrovertible fact!"

A most amazing thing happened next, a phenomenon that Buck-Teeth never in his life expected to witness. Kuro, grave Kuro—the Poet in Black—tossed back his head and roared with laughter!

"Tomorrow starts a new year, ninja," Buck-Teeth announced, happy tears freezing on his face. "I think I'll write a haiku!"

"I shall, also!" Kuro promised.

Shiro nodded vigorously.

And even tipsy Mido, the Poet in Green, watching the scene from his high, flowery perch in Buddha's Pure Land...concurred.

Everyone, except for the perplexed ninja, was howling now—including me, hunched over my paper-cluttered kitchen table in Mid-City, New Orleans. Our collective hilarity loosened a ponderous ledge of snow high above on the sacred mountain, and the avalanche came rumbling down.

It barely missed Kojiki and the poets but swept over and swallowed Nakamura, burying the critic for good.

AFTERWORD

ONCE AGAIN many thanks to Jim Kacian, editor extraordinaire, and to my writing group colleagues to whom this book is dedicated: Randolph Bates, Charles Gramlich, Michele Levy, and Patrice Melnick. I am also grateful to Josep Sobrer, who read and commented on an early draft—and to Kathleen Davis, my sharp-eyed proofreader.

Cup-of-Tea's character is based on the historical poet Issa, some of whose haiku appear in this book in translations based on texts found in *Issa Zenshû* [Nagano: Shinano Mainichi Shimbunsha, 1979]. Some haiku and translations were first published in *Issa: Cup-of-Tea Poems; Selected Haiku of Kobayashi Issa* [Asian Humanities Press, 1991], *Pure Land Haiku: The Art of Priest Issa* [Buddhist Books International, 2004], and in the prequel to this sequel, *Haiku Guy* [Red Moon Press, 2000].